WITCHCRAVEN

WITCHCRAVEN

Kate Dennis

This edition published in 2015 by Telos Moonrise:
Sinful Pleasures (An imprint of Telos Publishing)
5A Church Road, Shortlands, Bromley, Kent
BR2 0HP, United Kingdom

Telos Publishing values feedback if you have any
comments about this book please email
feedback@telos.co.uk

ISBN: 978-1-84583-919-2

British Library Cataloguing in Publication Data. A
catalogue record for this book is available from the
British Library.

1

Midnight.

In the old manor house at Witchcraven, Seraphina de Lacy slept between fine linen sheets. Her long dark hair spread over the pillows, her eyelashes fluttered, her red lips parted as she dreamed of her midnight lover. The dark, mysterious figure, his eyes passionate and demanding, let his gaze feast on her naked body. His glance lingered on her breasts, the curve of her waist, the slight mound of her stomach, then down to the triangle of dark hair between her thighs.

She grew moist. Her breath tightened, her legs fell open, parted, her back arched, thrusting her hips toward him as she longed for his touch. He leaned toward her. Stretched out his hand. One finger traced the line between her breasts down toward her hot and aching sex. She moaned, twisting in her sleep, while her dream lover bent his head. His lips brushed hers.

'It's time, my lady.'

'Oh yes,' she breathed. But the hand on her shoulder was not that of her lover. It was veined and old. The touch did not send shivers of pleasure racing through her blood, but rather shook her back into cold reality.

Seraphina opened her eyes to find Megan, her old nurse, smiling down at her.

'You dreamed?' the old woman grinned.

'I did, and much good did it do me.'

'It made you ready,' the old woman cackled. 'Come, get yourself off your back and on your feet. The night grows long and there is much to be done. Tonight you will become the true mistress of Witchcraven, just as your mother before you and your grandmother before her, and all the women of the manor stretching back into the mists of time have done. So come, my little one.'

Seraphina slid off the bed. A fire had been lit in the chamber, but the air on this midwinter night was still cold. Her skin prickled, her nipples, already aroused by her dream, stiffened. Taking one of the pink buds between her fingers, Megan pinched. A fierce, hard desire raced through Seraphina's veins, and she could not hold back the moan that escaped from her lips.

'Ripe, you are. Ripe,' the old woman cackled delightedly. 'I can smell your sex. I can feel your heat. Oh, you are a worthy offering to the horned one.'

Seraphina's stomach tightened. 'He will like me? He will take me?' she asked, an echo of doubt in her voice.

'He will revel in you,' Megan assured her. 'He will take his pleasure in your softness, he will blaze with your heat, thrust into your secret places with his tool until you will be transported into realms you could never have imagined. All you have to do is offer yourself to him, my little one. Remember that whatever you do on this night is what the Goddess demands of her followers, man and woman both.'

Seraphina drew in her breath and bowed her head.

'Now, now, there is no need to be afraid. All your life you have been preparing for this night. This is your destiny, your fate. Surrender to it and you will be the greatest of all the Ladies who have ruled over Witchcraven Manor. But we must hurry. The time is drawing near.'

With a little shrug, Seraphina slid her nightdress from her shoulders. Caressing her limbs, it slipped to the floor, and she stepped out of it onto the fur pelt that stretched in front of the fireplace. The flames crackled in the hearth, throwing their warm glow onto her white skin. Seraphina looked for the jug of hot water, the bowl in which she would wash herself, which Megan usually put close to the fire to keep warm.

The old woman shook her head. 'Tonight you will not wash. The Goddess demands the scent of your juices.'

Megan took a simple white shift that hung over a chair and slipped it over the girl's head. Then she lifted a heavy dark cloak from its peg and fastened it round her shoulders.

'Go with the Goddess, my little one,' Megan murmured, kissing the girl on the cheek. 'May you know the greatest of all pleasures in Her name.' She drew the hood of the cloak over Seraphina's head so that her face was completely hidden. 'They are waiting for you. Go silent and swift.'

Megan handed Seraphina a candle, then watched as the girl she had cared for since babyhood took the first step toward her appointed destiny.

Holding the candle high, Seraphina moved through the sleeping house. She stepped lightly down the old oak staircase, avoiding every familiar creak and groan in the timber, so that she passed as silent as a spectre into the flagged entrance hall then down the short corridor into the kitchen quarters. Copper pots and pans gleamed dimly in the candlelight. The fire was banked, the ashes glowing dully. The locks on the back door had been oiled and slid easily open.

As she stepped out into the cobbled yard, two figures moved out of the shadows. Like Seraphina, their faces were completely hidden, and their thick cloaks reached to the ground, so that it was impossible to tell whether they were male or female.

'I am here. Do with me what thou wilt,' Seraphina murmured the words Megan had told her she must say.

The figures bowed their heads. One took a strip of material and bound it round the girl's eyes, tightening it so that she could no longer see the moon that hung low over the hills or the stars that studded the winter sky. The other bound her hands behind her back with a leather thong. Then, still without a word, simply using the pressure of their hands on her arm to direct her, they led her out of the yard, through the ragged gardens of the manor and out into the wild land beyond.

Cold white fingers of moonlight splayed over rolling uplands. Deep in the clefts of the valleys, cottage doors were barred, their windows shuttered. Fires were banked high, candles set flickering on windowsills to chase away evil spirits. On this night of all nights, no-one who was not treading the upward path to the circle of standing stones, that dark brooding presence that dominated the surrounding countryside, would dare to leave the warmth and safety of their home. The Devil's Crown, the villagers called the stones. A place best avoided, especially at night. And even more so on a night such as this, All Hallow's Eve, when it was well known that restless souls wandered from their graves in search of those that in their lifetime had done them harm.

This was a superstition encouraged by the shadowed

figures that walked the dark paths that night, their shapes black against the whitened landscape, as they made their way toward the stone circle. They wanted no ignorant peasant or drunken lord to interrupt their rituals. Only those the Goddess had chosen were to be welcomed at the stones.

As Seraphina and her companions climbed higher, she became more aware of the coldness of the air; a keen, sharp cold that sliced through the thickness of her cloak and pinned the flimsy material of her shift around her body, outlining the curve of her hips, the roundness of her breasts. Her nipples, tightened and erect, strained against the thin material. The ground, laced with frost, was hard on her bare feet, and as the path narrowed and twisted unexpectedly, a projecting stone caught her foot. She stumbled and, with her bound hands and blindfolded eyes, would have fallen had not the two cloaked figures at her side steadied her. Her long dark hair streamed freely down her back as she walked, a willing victim, toward the dark circle of stones that loomed up in front of them on the crest of the hill.

The ground, as they neared it, flattened out. Seraphina felt the softness of grass beneath her feet and heard the faint whisper of the wind among the heather.

The moon was at its height now, casting its brilliance into the very centre of the circle, bleaching the ancient stones of their colour and throwing into dramatic relief the shrouded figures that stepped out from the shadows.

The worshippers gathered and formed a circle within a circle, surrounding the altar stone. Ten in number, their faces hooded and masked, they began to chant, a low, rhythmic, compelling chant. Guided by her companions, Seraphina stepped into the moonlight. In one quick movement her blindfold was removed and at the same time the leather thong cut from her wrists. She blinked against the sudden light.

'Bring forth the novice,' a woman's voice rang out.

The woman stood beside the altar stone. The upper part of her face was covered by an owl mask, there were wild leaves and berries tangled in her hair and her cloak had been thrown back from her shoulders, showing that she was completely naked.

Seraphina's guardians led her forward. With a sharp, harsh gesture they pulled her to the ground. For a moment her heart raced with fear. What if all she had been told by Megan was a lie? What if tonight she was not going to experience the greatest joy and pleasure of her life, but rather was going to be tortured and abused?

Forced onto her knees, she waited before the altar stone, her breath tight in her throat, her head spinning. The priestess stretched out her hand and touched her gently on her head, and the fear drained from her, like water running off a stone. Her voice was calm and strong as she gave her responses to the questions the priestess asked.

'Do you, maiden, untouched by man or woman, swear your allegiance to our Queen and Mother? Do you bring to her the sweet gift of your virginity?'

'I do. Willingly and without restraint.'

'If that is so indeed, and I do believe that it is, then from tonight you will be one of us. One of the chosen. Chosen by the Goddess to do her will. You will be with us. You will be part of us now and forever.'

'Now and forever,' came the refrain.

Taking her by the hand, the priestess raised Seraphina to her feet, then lent forward and kissed her on the mouth. Her lips were full and soft, her breath sweetened with wine and herbs that drowned the senses and sent the head spinning.

The stars seemed to whirl across the heavens, and the moon itself joined in their dance as the worshippers swooped down and seized Seraphina. She was thrust back onto the altar stone, her arms pinioned above her head, her legs spread wide. As she lay there stretched out to the moon and stars, the darkness of the night and the brooding power of the stones, a flash of silver danced about her head, then plunged toward her in one swift, sharp thrust.

Seraphina gasped. Her eyes closed, but she forced them open, determined to look, even if this was to be her last moment on Earth. In one clean movement from her navel to her throat, the knife cut through her shift, grazing the skin so that it left a thin trail of blood along the white flesh.

Other figures moved closer to the altar. The priestess lifted her head to the skies and cried, 'Sweet is the gift to our Queen, sweet indeed.'

An acolyte held up a chalice filled with blood-red wine, and the priestess held up the blood-smeared knife. The moonlight caught the stained steel. The watchers cried out. She plunged the weapon deep into the cup. The watchers moaned and sighed. They moved closer, their bodies touching, their breath coming faster, their arousal tangible as the priestess bent over the outstretched body.

Dipping her hand into the chalice, the priestess sprinkled the wine mixed with blood into Seraphina's mouth. Then, as the girl's lips closed over the sweet yet metallic taste, the priestess moved onto her breast, the rounded curve of her belly, and finally her melting, throbbing mound of Venus. Unable to stop herself, Seraphina raised her hips, offering herself and the passion that was beginning to build within her. The woman knelt at her head. Her long-fingered hands glided over the girl's white shoulders, her touch light as a feather, sending tingles of pleasure through Seraphina's veins, deepening the ache, the need in the pit of her stomach, sending the juices flowing. The woman's hand moved on. Down toward the firm white breasts. Resting lightly at first, her touch ignited every nerve and fibre of Seraphina's skin. Then, gently, softly, sweetly, the priestess began to stroke, until the waves of pleasure began to mount and Seraphina could not help but move, writhing on the cold stone as she chased her climax.

If she could, Seraphina would have reached down, pressed hard against her engorged clitoris; but firm hands held her down. Sharp nails seized her erect nipples, squeezing and pulling, sending wild currents of delight down to the throbbing centre between her legs. She cried aloud – she could not help herself – and the woman's hands moved downward, sliding over her ribcage, down over the stomach, kneading and stroking, her fingers curling the black tendrils of hair that covered her vagina. Then, as her labia opened, hot and wet and wanting, the priestess placed one hand on her stomach, letting it lie there, still and heavy, while her fingers lingered over the lips.

A touch. A single touch and she would come. Seraphina closed her eyes. She was almost there. Even without that connection she would come. The woman's hand moved away, and Seraphina bit hard on her lips to stifle the terrible cry of desire that forced its way into her throat. She ached, she longed, she throbbed with need. Trembled with desire, with a newly, desperately awakened hunger that threatened to engulf her.

At last unable to hold back any longer, she screamed,

'Take me. For the Goddess's sake, take me now!'

Her cry echoed round the stones. The hands that held her immobile melted away. She looked up, and he stood there before her, the mask of the horned god upon his head. He was naked but for the dark cloak flowing from his shoulders, and his erection was proud and fierce. Triumphantly he towered over her. He was everything she could ever want, everything she had ever desired, and she gave herself up totally, utterly to his domination. Yet at the same time, something deep within her knew that with her submission she too would achieve mastery.

With a cry she raised her arms in a gesture of surrender and triumph, and he entered her. She felt him hard and hot inside her, filling her, mentally as well as physically, so that she was aware of nothing but his cock. Her muscles tightened, squeezing hard as he began to move. Her rhythm matched his. The pain meant nothing – it added to the pleasure in a way she couldn't have imagined. He rose and fell with her, and each thrust brought her closer to the edge of climax. In her desperate need to reach that moment of sublime release, she clawed and scratched at his back. She writhed, she moaned, she screamed, while all around them the chant of the worshippers matched their rhythms, urging him on as he rode her, on and on to an eternity of pleasure until she came with such force that the world dissolved around her and all she knew was the endless wave after wave of orgasm.

At last, sweat-laden and spent, she lay panting on the altar stone. He rose from her, and the owl-masked woman came forward and knelt before him. Sweeping her cloak back from her shoulders to reveal her nakedness, the priestess took his member in her mouth.

He thrust his hips forwards and backwards, his hands raking her hair. As she sucked and licked, her hands curled round her breasts and she caressed her taut flesh. Her nipples grew hard and firm, and the watchers around her, aroused beyond control, threw off their cloaks. A young man, fair-haired and tall, held his cock in his hand. With a groan he sank to his knees behind the priestess. Grasping her buttocks he entered her. She moaned with pleasure, and her fingers tightened round her erect nipples. She swayed and groaned.

The girl on the altar stone sat upright. In front of her a woman stood, her back against a standing stone, her legs spread wide. A man knelt before her, his head between her thighs, his tongue licking, teasing at her clitoris. Rocking on her feet, she thrust her hips forward and came hard; and even as she cried out in her climax, he was on his feet and sliding his throbbing cock inside her. As he thrust into her, the woman's hands were on his firm, tight buttocks, caressing, smoothing, sliding down between his thighs, opening him up to the insistent penis of the worshipper wearing the mask of a bull.

Seraphina gasped. Watching them, the desire she had thought satisfied began to grow once more. She was hot. She was wet. The smell of the horned man's sex rose up to her nostrils, inflaming her further. Bracing her legs on either side of the altar, she rubbed herself against the cool stone. She must come. She must have more. She was throbbing, she was thrusting. If she were a man she would be coming already, spurting the hot, salty semen out onto the stone. Hot, damp, engorged, she cried out her need. Soft white hands encircled her waist. A touch of warm breath nuzzled her neck. A swathe of blonde hair fell over her shoulder. A girl's voice whispered in her ear: 'Come, let us worship the Goddess.'

She turned and found herself enfolded in an embrace. Soft breasts pressed against hers, hard hip bones thrust against hers. Small, cool hands cupped round her bottom, pulling her closer. Liquid now, melting with desire, Seraphina thrust herself against her seducer. The girl laughed, and deep blue eyes stared through the bird face of the mask she wore. Her lips found Seraphina's. Her kiss was warm and tender. Seraphina's mouth opened to her. The girl's tongue teased and withdrew. Seraphina's kisses became harder, more demanding. The girl laughed again and, taking one of Seraphina's hands in hers, guided her downwards. Their linked fingers touched soft curls, welcoming open labia and warm, sweet dampness. Even as Seraphina touched the forbidden cleft of another woman's body, she began to climax. The fair-haired girl drew in her breath and held her hand against Seraphina's swollen clitoris, pressing gently at first, then firmer until, with great shuddering gasps, Seraphina came against her fingers.

As the last wave engulfed her, she felt herself entered from behind by another of the worshippers. Falling onto her hands and knees, she lifted her head to the moon and cried out her pleasure. In front of her she saw the blue-eyed girl, her legs wide, her hips moving rhythmically, her cunt red and open, and she licked out her tongue and tasted her sweet juices as the girl writhed and moaned beneath her.

'Enough. You are mine. Remember that.' Her first lover, the man in the horned mask, lifted her up and laid her gently on the frosty grass. He spread his cloak over her and lay down beside her, covering them both with the thick dark material. His body was hard, well-muscled, and he smelled of sex and the wild wind and a deeper, muskier scent she knew was his alone. His arms were warm and they closed around her, holding her close. Her head on his chest, she could hear the steady beat of his heart. Although the ground was cold, his warmth spread through her. In his embrace, she felt so loved and safe. Her limbs grew loose and relaxed. Her eyes closed.

Just as she was drifting into a sated sleep, he shifted his weight. Leaning on one elbow, he moved his head downwards, his lips searching, nuzzling, then fastening onto her nipple. With a sigh of pleasure, he began to suck, and out of the deep relaxation into which her body had fallen, Seraphina felt the first stirring not only of desire, but of something else. A feeling of warmth and rightness she had never known before.

'My love,' she murmured as his lips sucked and pulled at her breast. 'My only love.'

His cock grew against her stomach. She smiled and curled her fingers around it, her hand lazily moving up and down. He shivered. He moved from one nipple to the next and, feeling totally in control, she guided him inside her. He lay there very still. Only his mouth moved. She squeezed her thighs together, feeling him fill her.

They lay there for a while, totally content. Then his hands slid round her buttocks and, still inside her, his cock as hard as the stone she had lain on, he lifted her up, holding her impaled on his member.

The first tremors of her orgasm made Seraphina gasp. Unable to help herself, she sank her nails into his shoulders and threw back her head, her long, silky hair caressing her naked back as they rocked backwards and forwards. Each movement sent him deeper inside her, intensifying her every sensation, growing her orgasm, feeding her pleasure until at last she could no longer hold back. Sinking deep onto him, she let herself go. Her whole body shook and vibrated. She was flying, her head was in the stars, her body floating high above the moonlit landscape.

'My love. My lady, my love.'

Did she hear him say those words, or had she imagined them?

Her eyes shut. Totally replete and satisfied, she let herself slide away into sleep. Gently, tenderly he freed himself. Taking his cloak, he wrapped it around himself, becoming once more a mysterious, godlike figure, and slipped away into the shadows of the night.

The icy air cooled Seraphina's hot skin. A hand traced an ancient blessing on her forehead. Strong arms lifted her. A warm cloak was pulled around her. Held firm, her cold flesh warmed by another's heat, she was carried from the circle.

2

Seraphina woke in her own bed, stretching out on the soft feather mattress that enclosed her in a warm nest. She thought for a moment that the previous night had been no more than the dream that came to her night after night; but this time the dream had come to its longed-for ending. At last she had had her mysterious lover and tasted the utter and complete bliss of giving herself to him. And there had been more. He had pleasured her, but she in turn had pleasured him.

Seraphina smiled in satisfaction and cuddled down under the covers, enjoying the feeling of crisp fresh sheets against her skin, the scent of lavender that hung about her pillow.

A thin shaft of winter sunlight threaded through the mullioned window, revealing the familiar bedroom. The low-beamed ceiling, the worn rug on the floor before the now empty hearth. Surely last night there had been a fire? Or had it been only in her dream? Seraphina shook her head. It must have been in her dream, because a fire was a luxury they could ill afford.

Her breath rose into the air. She burrowed further under her blankets and caught the rich scent of her own body, the musky tang of her juices, but also the sharp smell of those who had penetrated her. So it had not been a dream. It had really happened. The owl-masked woman, the girl with the blue eyes and the horned god, who had brought with him the overwhelming feeling of love and being loved, and with it the certainty that he was her eternal partner.

Seraphina sighed with remembered joy, then buried her head beneath the covers and curled her arms around her sated body. Like her lover's arms, her warmth enfolded her, comforting and soothing. She yawned. Her eyes closed and she drifted back into her dreams.

She was back in the circle. White moonlight on black stone, bodies on bodies, writhing, twisting, striving. Naked faces, strange and powerful. Flesh on her flesh, stroking, caressing, thrusting until her body flooded with pleasure. She woke with a moan. Megan had been right: it was like nothing she had ever experienced before. Utter and complete bliss, total satisfaction.

Lithe as a cat, she slipped out from between the warm sheets and stood naked in the chill air. Her body glowed in the dim light, breasts erect, nipples hard. Her dark hair flowed down her back. Shaking her head, she felt the tresses soft and sensual across her shoulders.

The door opened. Megan, dressed in her usual black, came in carrying a tray on which stood a silver goblet. She placed the tray on the chest beside the window and took Seraphina's hand in hers.

'Welcome into your womanhood, my lady,' she murmured.

'You prepared me well.' Seraphina bowed her head and kissed the wrinkled cheek.

Megan had cared for her since her mother had died when she was a baby. At the old woman's side she had learned the ancient knowledge and ritual, so that when the time came she could take her rightful place in the worship of the Goddess at the stone circle.

As long as there had been a manor house at Witchcraven, its mistress had practiced the occult arts, and the lands had passed down through the female side. Few boys were ever born into the family, and those that were, were generally sickly, or if they grew up to be strong young men, went abroad in search of their fortune and never came back, leaving their sisters to inherit.

'You are the Lady of the Mysteries,' the old woman said, and Seraphina gave her a quick hug. 'And the most beautiful,' her nurse continued.

Seraphina frowned. Had her old nurse been there in the scared stone circle? Had she too worn a mask and copulated naked under the moon? She opened her mouth to ask, then shut it again, knowing that from now on she must question no-one close to her. Those who wished to be revealed as followers of the Goddess would be revealed. For others, the exposure of their true allegiance would be so dangerous that no-one must ever know that they followed the old, forbidden ways.

'Here, drink this.' Megan poured a thick black liquid into the glass goblet and held it to Seraphina's lips.

The liquid tasted of wormwood and ashes, and was so harsh and bitter that at the first sip Seraphina's gorge rose and her stomach heaved. But her nurse held the goblet to her mouth until she had drained it. As the last drops slid down her throat, a searing heat shot through her limbs. The sweat stood on her forehead and her stomach cramped. Pressing her hands against her belly, she gasped aloud at the sudden pain.

'Aye, that's right, my little lady. The drug will let it go, so shake it free. After this there will be no child to lodge in your womb. No babe to tear your flesh and break your nights and torment your days. Not until you wish it will you bear the next Lady of Witchcraven.'

'It hurts,' Seraphina groaned.

'Only for a moment. See, already it passes.'

The old woman went to the bowl of water that stood on the chest. She dipped a piece of rag into it and placed the chilled cloth on the girl's forehead.

'There, there,' she soothed, and even as she spoke, the pain eased. The cramps lessened into a dull ache in Seraphina's back and a slight tension in the thighs. Then her limbs relaxed and the pain was gone.

'There will be a visitor to the manor today,' Megan continued with that infallible knowledge of what was to be, that she had displayed since the little Seraphina had been first able to understand. 'I'll bring out your good silk, but first you must wash.'

The girl went to the basin and plunged her hands into icy water. Cupping her fingers, she splashed her face and neck. Then, taking the rag the old woman had used to mop her brow, she wet it once more and rubbed it over her breasts. The skin tingled, and she smiled as she smoothed the cloth over her stomach and down between her legs.

Megan brought petticoats of finest cotton, which she slipped over Seraphina's head. Then she laced her young mistress into a boned linen corset that narrowed her waist and pushed up her high white breasts. Finally there came the dress itself, of a heavy ivory-coloured silk, embroidered with a pattern of red flowers and green leaves. Its sleeves were trimmed with frothy lace and its neck cut low over the half-naked breasts, which were slightly veiled by a scarf of the finest lawn.

When she was dressed, Seraphina sat on a low stool

while her hair was swept up above her forehead and pinned up on the top of her head, with one long curl left to fall seductively onto her breast. She wore no jewellery but a single pearl drop in one ear, and round her neck she tied a narrow ribbon of black velvet.

'There you are. As beautiful as our lady your mother. I can see her power in you,' Megan declared.

With a rustle of silk, Seraphina crossed to the mirror that hung like a pure silver oval beside her bed. She gazed at herself, looking to see how she had changed from the untouched virgin of the day before; but, unaware of the aura of sexuality that now hung about her, she could see nothing different in the green eyes that looked back at her. All she knew was that her stomach was growling with hunger.

'Hurry down to the parlour and I'll bring you something to break your fast,' her nurse said.

'And my father, will he be joining me?'

'Oh no, my dearest, he is long gone out about some business or other.' Megan's expression showed what she felt about her master.

Seraphina released a sigh. She had no wish to see her father, whom she detested. Sir Greville cared only for his horses and dogs and had no time for his only child. What was worse, he had no interest in his estate, and Seraphina, who had been taught from her earliest days that the lands of Witchcraven were hers to hold and care for throughout her life, was angered by the way he had spent his income freely on what interested him while leaving his tenant farmers with leaking roofs and undrained fields. In the past few years some land had been sold off to pay gambling debts, leaving the future Lady of Witchcraven to wonder if there would be anything left of the estate when the day came for her to take up her inheritance. The anger and frustration she felt over her father's stupidity and irresponsible attitude made it almost impossible for her to remain in the same room as him, so her heart was light with relief at his absence as she ran down the stairs to the parlour.

She ate hungrily. Sharp white teeth tearing into the bread and cheese. Red lips sucking thirstily at the cool brown ale. Hunger and thirst satisfied, she moved from the table and settled herself on the window seat. Tucking her feet under her skirts, she leaned back against the old oak panelling and wondered what the day would bring. A clatter of hooves on the cobbles below interrupted her daydreams. She sat up, startled.

'That'll be your cousin Harry, never you fear,' Megan said as she cleared the dishes from the table. The younger son of Sir Greville's sister, young, strong and handsome Harry was a favourite of the old woman's. 'He'll make you a fine husband, give you a strong daughter,' she continued.

It was the nurse's dearest hope that one day the cousins would marry. Until last night, it had been something that Seraphina had wanted too. Now, as she remembered the horned man's lovemaking at the stones, she was no longer so sure. Harry was attractive and fun, but her midnight lover was the one man she could bind herself to for all eternity. Just thinking about him made her warm and moist. But he was not here. She did not even know who he was, and there was no way of finding out. So in the meantime she might as well make use of her cousin.

Seraphina pressed her face against the thick glass of the mullioned window. Outside, the courtyard was empty.

'That will be him,' Megan repeated.

Seraphina shook her head. 'Give me my book,' she said.

The old woman passed her a book of etchings of local sights, and Seraphina turned the pages with impatient fingers until she came to a picture of the Devil's Crown. Holding the book on her lap, she stared at the grainy picture. In this representation the stones were all of an equal shape and size, linked by a plinth that ran the full circumference of the circle. Flaming torches had been stuck into sconces, and even this black-and-white picture was lit by a weird brilliance that illuminated the long-bearded, white-robed druid, mistletoe branch in hand, who stood at the altar stone declaiming his prayers to his god.

Seraphina being aware of the true nature of the worship at the stones, this picture rarely failed to bring a scornful smile to her lips. Today however her mind was on other matters. Megan had said that cousin Harry would call. Her father and his mother were brother and sister, and both had married well, but where Sir Greville had wasted most of his money, Lady Harriet's husband had not. Seraphina was poor, Harry was rich – or would be, on the death of his father.

In spite of the difference in their circumstances, the two children had played together when they were little, and Seraphina, who was slightly older, could always dominate her impressionable cousin. Now however they were both grown up. Harry had been away at school and had seen and learned far more than she had, which she found exciting and stimulating. Before last night, she would have said she was in love with him. Now she was less certain. However, if she had to marry someone to make sure that Witchcraven would survive, and if she could not have her horned man, Harry would be the one she would choose.

'You have the power,' Megan said, reading her thoughts. 'All you have to do is use it.'

Seraphina's red lips curved upwards, her green eyes shone. 'I will use it,' she whispered. 'I will.'

At her words, the room grew very still, as if the air itself was holding its breath. There was a long moment of silence, then Megan went over to the log basket and, taking a handful of pine cones, threw them onto the fire. They sputtered and sparked, then burst into flame, filling the parlour with their resinous scent, as Harry Fitzgerald burst into the room.

Harry's face was flushed, alive with the pleasure of a wild ride over the hills, and his fair hair flopped over his forehead. He was boyishly handsome, with broad shoulders, long legs and a tight behind, and his energy flowed into the room. Seraphina dropped her eyes. Her long, dark lashes fluttered as she bent her head over her book.

One long curl of black hair snaked round her white neck and fell enticingly onto her high white breasts, which rose and fell above her tightly-laced bodice with every breath. She moved a little and her petticoats lifted, revealing a glimpse of a white ankle under the flurry of cotton and silk. She heard Harry swallow and knew that he had never seen her like this before.

Taking her time, well aware of the effect she was having on her cousin, Seraphina finally looked up. Green eyes met brown. The book slipped from her lap and she made no attempt to retrieve it. She simply did not move; rather, her glance locked into his, forcing him to come closer.

'Harry.' Her voice was soft as a sigh as she held out her hand. Trembling, he took it and lifted her long, white fingers to his lips. She felt his hot mouth on her cool skin, his lips lingering far longer than was polite, and she curled her fingers round his, pressing her nails into the palm of his hand.

She said his name again as she slipped to her feet, and his breath came quick and fast. She was standing very close to him now. She turned her face up toward his, her lips slightly parted, aware of his arousal. Her green eyes dared, invited, seduced. Recklessly he pulled her close, and she felt the hardness of his male body against the soft white flesh of her half-naked breasts. He groaned as she pressed herself against him, straining toward him as her lips brushed his and his mouth came down hard on hers.

They kissed, eagerly, hungrily. Clinging almost desperately to each other, he hard against her, she wet and ready. His hands slid down her back, encircling her buttocks as she leaned against the panelled wall.

'Yes,' she whispered, all restraint gone. 'Oh yes.'

The power of her passion surged within her. Her desire inflamed his. His hands fumbled for her breasts, her fingers searched for his buttons. His fingers found her nipples. Her hand closed around his penis. He bent his head and began to suck. She raked her fingers through his hair and, moaning with the pleasure that shot through her body, squeezed his throbbing cock. Her thumb stroked the shaft, her fingers caressed the tip and felt the first salty bead of his juice upon her skin.

Her mouth watered. She longed to kneel before him, to lick him into an ecstasy of pleasure. She tried to twist free, but he held her firm, pressed hard against the panelling. His hands searched frantically through her skirts, pulling up her petticoats until she stood exposed, showing the dark triangle of hair between her smooth, firm thighs. Her juices flowed from her, her cunt pulsed. Digging her nails into his shoulder, she cried out her need. He thrust toward her. Her eyes closed, legs spread wide open, poised on the edge of release.

'Now,' she whispered. 'Take me now.'

Rough hands seized her. A ringing blow to the head sent her spinning to the floor.

'You bitch! You whore! Is this how you behave the moment I turn my back?'

Purple-faced with rage, Sir Greville swung his riding crop at Harry. 'As for you, you lecherous young pig, get yourself out of here and never let me catch you with my daughter again!'

'Papa!' Seraphina sprang to her feet, eyes blazing, as Sir Greville raised his whip above his nephew's shoulder. 'Stop!' she cried.

Sir Greville's fingers trembled. The muscles of his arms went limp and the whip dropped from his grasp. Shaken, he stared in disbelief into his daughter's furious green eyes. 'I'll beat you too, miss,' he faltered uncertainly.

'Seraphina.' Harry put himself between them.

'No, Harry. You go. I am all right. Don't worry about me. Never worry about me.' She smiled at him quickly.

'I'll not let him hurt you,' Harry cried.

'He won't, don't you worry.' Seraphina shook her head, then mouthed silently, 'Meet me in the usual place.'

He hesitated, but she nodded briefly, and at last, to her relief, he left.

'Aye, send him on his way, girl,' Sir Greville said. 'He's not for you. I've better things in mind for my only daughter.'

Seraphina's nostrils flared. She drew herself up to her

full height and, eyes blazing, faced her father. 'I do as I wish, and no-one, least of all you, will stop me,' she said.

Scarlet with rage, Sir Greville lunged toward his daughter, but Seraphina did not give way. She held up her hand and, to her surprise, her father, like a horse pulled tight on the rein, juddered to a halt.

For a moment he seemed confused, bewildered, and she had to hide her smile as he finally managed to stammer, 'You are my daughter and you'll do as I say.'

Then he turned and lumbered out of the room.

'No, I don't think so,' Seraphina hissed after his retreating back. She was not going to give way to her father, on this or on anything – not anymore, not now she had come into her womanhood. But how was she going to get what she wanted?

3

'I am my own woman and I will do as I please,' Seraphina told herself furiously. 'My *father* –' she spat out the word '– has no right to tell me what to do. I go my own way, the way of all the Ladies of Witchcraven, and he goes his.'

She paced the parlour, seething with anger at the pathetic man who tried to pretend he had some control over her, and at a world that gave such men power over women. As she walked, her skirts swayed round her hips, but the fine cotton of her petticoats caught between her legs. Like any lady of her class, she wore no drawers, and aroused by her anger and the unfinished business with her cousin, she felt the material of her petticoats bunch up between the swelling lips of her vagina. She took a step, and the cotton rubbed, tantalisingly, excruciatingly pleasurable. Another step, and excitement coiled like a spring within her. Slipping her hand under the bodice of her dress, she let her fingers play with her nipple. Instantly it rose, straining hard against the silk, inflaming her further. Her thighs rubbed against each other, slippery with her dampness. Her breathing quickened. She was on the edge. Another step or two and she would bring herself off, but could she wait?

Half falling onto the window seat, she knelt facing the cool green glass of the window. With frantic hands, she pulled aside her skirts and thrust a finger into her warm, wet darkness. Her muscles tensed. Holding her breath, she braced herself for the pleasure that would come. Squeezing her nipples hard, she moved her finger to her clitoris, throbbing, pulsating. She stroked, she rubbed, she squeezed until the climax exploded within her. Wave upon wave of pleasure shook her until at last, exhausted, she leaned her flushed face against the windowpane.

Her breath misted the glass as her breathing calmed. Arching her back, she stretched out her arms and almost purred with the satisfaction she had given herself. If she had been a cat, she would have curled up there on the window seat and slept the afternoon away. Not being a cat, she had other matters to attend to. Her cousin Harry for one.

He would be waiting for her at their usual place, and she must not delay much longer, for if she did not get to him soon, he would think that she was not coming. She had to see him. She had to show him that without a shadow of a doubt, she was the only woman for him. If her father was going to be difficult and put obstacles in their way, Harry must be strong enough to stand up against him. His own father would not be happy about their union either. He would want his son and heir to make a much better match than his impoverished cousin, however beautiful she was. Seraphina gave herself a pleased little shake. She was beautiful, but more than that, she was powerful, and she must use that power to bind Harry to her for all time; for if she could not have the lover who came to her in her dreams, the man in the mask of the horned god who had taken her in the sacred ritual of the Goddess, then she would have her charming, handsome, innocent cousin, and would mould him to her will.

She stood up. She shook out her skirts. She lifted her finger to her nose and smelled the scent of her juices on her skin. She was ready. Taking a smooth, rosy apple from the bowl of fruit on the table, she fetched her cloak and went into the stable yard. Talking to the groom, she discovered that her father, as she had hoped he would, had taken his hunter out for one of his mad gallops across the moorland. Whenever Sir Greville's temper could not be cooled by a swift kick or a harsh beating, especially when whoever he wanted to intimidate stood up to him, he would have his horse saddled and ride for as many hours as it took to calm his fury. Then, when at last his anger had gone, he would find his way to the nearest tavern and drink himself insensible. Sometime later that night, or even the next morning, the innkeeper would have him put on his horse and the animal would take him home.

'The Goddess grant it will be an all-night affair,' Seraphina murmured as she passed the hunter's empty stall. 'For I, Great Lady of the Moon and Tides, am about your business and need no interference from a drunken sot of an unbeliever such as my miserable father.'

She cast a quick glance in the direction she was going to take, and sent up another swift prayer that Sir Greville was already far away. Taking the apple from the pocket of her skirt, she rubbed it against the top of her thigh, relishing the sensation of the hard fruit on her supple flesh, before offering it to the mare that looked at her with soft brown eyes over the top of her stall.

When the animal had finished, she stroked her velvety nose, leaning her face against the firm neck and breathing in the scent of horse. Then she called for the stable boy to saddle up the mare.

'Be quick about it, if you please,' she murmured in the low, husky voice that she knew would send the lad scurrying to carry out her orders far quicker than any sharp request.

As soon as the mare was saddled, the boy led her to the mounting block and held the stirrup for his mistress. With a billow of skirts, Seraphina seated herself on the horse's back, allowing the boy a glimpse of slim white ankle as she did so. She smiled inwardly as she saw his reaction. Half worship, half lust, it was just what she wanted. From now on, if ever she needed a horse made ready, then there would be one person who would hurry to do her bidding.

'Thank you,' she whispered, leaning down toward him, her cloak falling open, her half-naked breasts threatening to fall out of her tightly-laced bodice. The boy almost fell backwards in awe and arousal.

'Naughty boy to show me what you have hidden in your britches,' Seraphina murmured, licking her tongue over her lips. 'And such a size, too.' Then she straightened up and rode out of the yard, leaving the boy staring open-mouthed and erect behind her.

Once free of the house and grounds, she urged her horse into a gallop. The air was crisp and fresh; the wind took her hair, blowing it out behind her. The winter sun at this time of year was low on the horizon, streaking the uplands with long fingers of light as Seraphina rode up the twisting path. High on the ridge above her were the gnarled shapes of the Devil's Crown. The ancient stones were mottled with lichens and mosses, echoing the colours of gorse and heather that cloaked the hillside. Seraphina however had no business with the stones. She guided her mare along a lower slope to where the ground dipped suddenly into a cleft between two rocks.

This secret place, hidden from passing eyes by the overhanging rocks, was where she and Harry had played as children. Then it had been battles fought with sticks as swords and bows made from wood and string. Or they had pretended to sail away to some far-distant land where strange creatures such as dragons and camelopards roamed and they had to fight the natives for their very survival. Another favourite was being captured by pirates on the Caribbean Sea. Harry liked to be the pirate captain, the wicked Blackbeard, and she was the maiden he had captured and was holding to ransom. Sometimes her evil guardian refused to find the gold and she would be forced to walk the plank. Seraphina would stand on the very edge of the rock, one foot suspended over the thin air, waiting for the moment when the pirate captain would be defeated by her noble cousin Sir Harry, who would rescue her from his wicked clutches and carry her away to some far-distant island where they would reign happily as king and queen for the rest of their lives.

In all these games Harry thought he was taking the lead role, and Seraphina let him believe it, whereas in fact it was she who thought up the stories, who invented even more terrible dangers, who decided which mythical creature would die and which would prove to be their loyal friend. Sometimes she would even suggest that this time she would be the noble hero and save Harry from danger; and sometimes, greatly daring, he would agree. On those occasions he would be rewarded by more than the usual kiss he got for freeing her from a dastardly pirate or fire-breathing dragon. When she rescued Harry, the grateful victim was in her control, and if her fingers lingered when untying him from the dungeon into which he had been thrown, if her hands strayed between his legs, to close around the thickness of his cock as it strained at his breeches, then who was there to see, or to blame her? And if, when she had teased and sent him home, she felt the need to sit down on the sandy floor of the cleft and release the tension between her thighs, then only the kestrel whirling high above her head would hear her gasps of pleasure.

Seraphina cast a glance at the sky, but no bird of prey rode the wind. There would be no witness to what was going to happen there that day. A frisson of excitement tingled between her legs. She pressed her thighs together, enjoying the sensation. This was why ladies rode side-saddle, she thought, biting her lip against any further arousal. She should save herself for him, and time was running short. Sliding slowly and sensuously from the back of her horse, she took the reins and led the mare down between the rocks into the shelter of the cleft. Protected from the buffeting wind, it was strangely still and quiet.

Harry was waiting for her. He had tethered his horse and was sitting on a boulder, shoulders slumped, staring gloomily into the far distance. The sandy floor muffled the sound of her mare's hoof beats, but as they approached the miserable young man, the animal whickered softly, and Harry spun round. When he saw who it was, he jumped to his feet.

'Seraphina, thank the Lord. I thought your father …'

'Never,' she interrupted. 'He may growl and bluster all he wants, but I do as I will.'

He moved toward her and would have pulled her into his arms and kissed her, but she stepped back.

'Not yet.'

She lifted a finger to her lips and, sticking out her tongue, ran it along the length of the digit. Tasting herself, she half closed her eyes and stood watching from under her eyelashes as her cousin groaned and swayed toward her. 'I told you. We have time.' Coming closer, she pressed the moistened finger against his lips. He groaned again. Curving his mouth against it, he sucked it in. His lips moved up and down, mimicking the action he wanted her to perform, but she stood passive, smiling, hiding her own arousal, until at last, unable to bear it any longer, he grabbed her by the wrist and forced her hand between his legs.

'Oh Harry, this is what we did when we were children,' she sighed. 'Do you remember?' In spite of herself, her own breath was coming faster now.

'God's teeth,' he groaned. 'Seraph, if you don't do me now, I'll come in my britches.'

She wanted to delay, to prolong the tease, but she could feel him tense beneath her grip. Quickly she undid his buttons, releasing the engorged cock. Proud and scarlet it stood erect. Her fingers tightened round it and she lowered her head, but before her mouth could reach him, he came in vast, violent spurts all over her hand.

'I'm –' he began. But she would not let him finish. Fastening her lips on his, she kissed him deep and hard. For a moment he did not react, then he thrust into her mouth with his tongue. Hot and wet, at the taste of him she ground her hips into his, pressed her pulsating centre against the hardness of his body.

'Give me a second and I'll be up for it,' he said hoarsely.

'I would, if I could, but I can't,' she gasped. 'I'll come whether you touch me or not. But feel me, Harry. Feel me, and I'll come all the better.'

Her eyes widened, her breasts heaved, her legs parted. His hand was in her skirts. He was fumbling his way to her clitoris, but she could not wait. Taking his fingers, she pressed them to her.

'God,' she heard him say as she exploded in a tidal wave of pleasure.

'Goddess,' she echoed, swaying against him, her breasts against his chest, her cunt against his hand, draining every last second of sensation from his firm, well-muscled body.

Even as she subsided against him, she felt his cock harden against her thigh. Closing her eyes, she let her breathing resume its normal rhythm while deciding what she would do next. This coupling was an echo of their childhood experiments, and while it pleasured them both, it was not enough to bind them – or to enslave him and make sure that he would be with her when she defied her father's wishes.

'Wait,' she whispered. 'Not yet. I must recover from the force of your coming. You are so strong Harry, so virile. I am –' she fluttered her lashes before half closing her eyes and murmuring, '– a little afraid of what you might do to me.'

'Zounds, Seraph, you know I would not hurt you. For all the world I would never do you any damage.'

'You might not, my brave and handsome cousin, but he might.' Seraphina cast a provocative glance at his fully extended member. 'He is so large, I fear he will split my very being in two.'

'You mean –?' Harry stopped as if he could not believe what she was suggesting.

'What else?' She swayed toward him. 'We have waited so long, far too long. This morning when you left, I was distraught. I knew then that I needed you, I had to have you, that I would never rest until you had filled me to the utmost. But please, please, when you do, when you thrust him inside me with all your force, do not hurt me.' She gazed up at him, her emerald eyes sparkling with tears, her lower lip trembling. 'Or, at least, do not hurt me more than you and he –' she let her hand graze the engorged member '– can manage to avoid.'

Catching hold of her wrist, Harry groaned with pent-up desire. He would have guided her hand to his throbbing cock, but she pulled away.

'Not like this. I told you. Today it will be as it should. It will be man and woman together, not boy and girl. We will be lovers, Harry, not childhood sweethearts finding our innocent way through forbidden delights. We will take each other with full knowledge and consent to what we do.'

'You mean us to swear our vows – undying love, being together forever and all that?' There was a frown on his face, and a reluctant note to his voice that made her wonder if she'd gone too far.

To keep him, set him free. The voice in her head was so clear that for a second she wondered if there was someone stood there beside him. She glanced over his shoulder, but they were alone. Looking upwards through the canopy of overhanging rock, however, she could just see one of the ancient stones that lined the long-lost way to the circle. *My thanks to you, my Mother, my Goddess*, she thought. *You have shown me what I must do.* Mouthing a quick kiss, she stepped away from Harry. She lifted her arm and, tossing her head, let her hair sweep over her shoulders. Then she laughed.

'Oh Harry, how you mistake me,' she said softly. 'You and I have known each other since we were babes in arms. We don't need to make each other any promises. Do we?'

His face cleared, he grinned, and she took his hand in

hers. Lifting it to her lips, she kissed it. Softly at first, a caress as light as thistledown, then moving her lips in a series of butterfly kisses. He trembled beneath her touch. She smiled to herself, her mouth hidden as she worked her way along to his fingers, hesitated, then took the longest into her mouth and sucked.

His eyes closed, his hips thrust toward her, member erect. Letting go of his hand, she slid to her knees and took him in her mouth. Her tongue lapping round the pulsing cock, she sucked, tasted the salty, briny taste; but before he could come, she let him go.

'No,' he groaned.

'Yes,' she laughed. 'Oh yes.' And with a swirl of her skirts she turned from him. His hands fell on her waist, and for a moment she thought she had misjudged and he would pull her to him and ravage her from behind, but when she stepped forward, he let her go.

'Not here,' she said as lightly as she could, and led him to the deepest shadow.

Then, sinking gracefully onto the soft, sandy floor, she lifted her skirts and held out her arms. Letting her legs fall open, she raised her hips, and then he was on her, thrusting deep inside her while she moved with him, matching his rhythm, building and building toward the climax. She was there, she was almost there, when with a great shout he came.

Stranded on the edge, she wanted to scream, to scratch, to pull at his hair; but knowing she must not do anything to anger or upset him, she slid her hand into her secret place and, with a quick pressure, released her orgasm.

'Oh,' she sighed. 'That was wonderful, beyond words.' She sighed again and, lifting her head, kissed him lightly on the lips.

'I made you come,' he grinned, looking so pleased with

himself that she did not know whether she wanted to hit or hug him. Before she could decide, he had moved to one side and, with a great yawn, settled himself on the sandy floor. His head on her breast, he pulled his cloak around them. His eyes closed, and within minutes he was asleep.

Seraphina sat and watched him. His skin was fair and she could see the blue veins in his eyelids, the sandy lashes that fringed his eyes, the glow on his cheeks. His breathing was deep and easy. His lips were red, his hair flopped over his forehead and made him look for all the world like a little boy. She lifted her hand to push the fringe gently back from his eyes, bent her head to kiss his cheek, as if he were her child. The thought stopped her in mid action. A cold shudder coiled in the pit of her stomach. She half closed her eyes and, catching her lip in her teeth, she chewed it in a mixture of anger and anxiety.

What had she done? What had she committed herself to? Of course she loved her cousin. She had known him since childhood. She was easy and comfortable in his presence and, what was even more important, knew that she could make him do exactly as she desired. But was this a quality she wanted in a husband?

Seraphina shook her head violently. Harry half woke, and she absently stroked his hair. He settled back again, slipping into an even deeper sleep. Seraphina drew in her breath. Furious with herself, she fought back the urge to tip him onto the ground, jump on the back of her mare and gallop wildly across the uplands until her heart stopped beating so fast and she was calm again.

You're just like your father, she inwardly reproached herself. *Useless, stupid, acting before you think.*

Her shoulders slumped, and angry tears rose to her eyes. As she blinked them away, she looked up and saw the first faint trace of the moon sailing above the swirling clouds.

'Goddess, save me from myself,' she prayed. 'Show me the way in which I might still do *thy* wish.'

A wisp of cloud veiled the outline of the moon. The skies seemed to darken, then the wind rose in a long, slow sweep and the moon was revealed. It shone brighter now. Closer. Almost touching the rocks above their head. Even though she knew it was not possible, Seraphina felt that she could almost reach up and touch its silver surface, and that if she did so she would be blessed and comforted by the lady she worshipped. A feeling of warmth and calm washed over her. She had not failed. Whatever plan the Goddess had for her, making love to her cousin had not destroyed it.

Seraphina cast a quick glance at Harry's innocent, open face. Could it be that he was part of what was destined? His mother was her father's sister. Could she also be a worshipper of the Goddess? Sir Greville had said that Harry's parents would be against their marriage, but had he asked Harry's mother? Had anyone? Women in this world were seldom consulted about anything the men in their lives considered important.

Seraphina wriggled herself into a more comfortable position and tried to think what she knew about her aunt. It was not helpful. Lady Harriet was very much like her brother. Her greatest passions in life, after her sons - for Harry was the eldest of four - were her dogs and her horses. She liked nothing better than to go hunting, and when she could not, she spent her time in her kennels with her dogs, or poring over her stud books to decide which animal should be mated with which. This was not a woman who interested herself either in herbal lore or medicine, or anything spiritual at all. She went to the parish church with her husband and sons every Sunday, but as far as Seraphina knew, she slept through much of the parson's sermon. Or at least she sat in her pew with her eyes closed, and an occasional grunt left her lips.

The thought of her aunt or any of her family taking part in the wild lovemaking at the stones was ridiculous, Seraphina decided. So, must she make her stand alone, with no-one but Harry to take her part when she defied both their families? Would he be strong enough? She looked down at her sleeping cousin. As if he sensed her glance, his lips curved into a smile and he moved his head against her breast, then sighed with such contentment and satisfaction that he looked as if he could stay there all night.

The light, however, was fading rapidly, and if she was not home soon then her absence would be noted. At least her father would not be there, but Megan might fret and even send someone out to look for her, and it was best that she was not found, here in this place with her cousin. Even a casual passerby could be a threat. With her wild hair and the scent of Harry's juices on her, there would be no doubt about what they had been doing, and if she wanted to present herself to his parents as a suitable wife, then she had to look as if she were a virgin.

At the thought of appearing innocent and naïve, Seraphina laughed out loud, and this finally woke Harry. He opened his eyes and stared at her, startled.

'What? Where?' he muttered blearily.

'Here, with me, my love.' Seraphina made her voice low and husky. 'You made love to me, Harry. You gave me great, great pleasure,' she murmured, half closing her eyes and letting her hand stray to his chest.

Her fingers slid under his shirt and teased at his nipple. He groaned and made to reach for her, but she immediately withdrew her hand and shrank back from him. 'It was beyond anything I could have hoped for, blissful, heavenly, but we must go.'

'Yes, I suppose we must. It's getting late, and cold. Come on, let me help you up.'

They stood up and she swayed toward him, her eyes filling with tears as she whispered, 'Oh Harry, don't let them part us.'

'Part us? Never! I am yours, Seraph, forever and a day.' He drew her close and kissed her tenderly.

'But what about our families? You know how my father feels about you. Given his way, he would have whipped you out of the house.'

'He thinks I'm not good enough for you,' Harry said miserably. 'And he might be right. You are the most wonderful creature that ever trod this Earth. You are far, far too good for the likes of a clodhopping idiot like me.'

'No!' Seraphina opened her eyes wide. Her lower lip trembled and her voice shook as she said, 'You must never, never let him make you think that. You are my dearest, dearest cousin. We have known and loved each other since we were children. Our parents are kin. How can you possibly not be good enough for me? Far rather –' and here taking a risk and crossing her fingers, she went on – 'your family will think I'm not good enough for you. After all, I do not have much of a dowry. All I will have is the manor of Witchcraven, when my father dies.'

'Money! What does that matter, to true lovers like us?' Harry cried boldly.

She'd got him! Triumph and relief swept through Seraphina. She would marry her cousin in spite of anything her father would do or say, and so follow a long and sacred tradition. The Ladies of Witchcraven never bowed to any man. Rather they bent the men in their lives to their will. And their will was always for the greater good of the Goddess.

Throwing her arms around Harry's neck, she kissed him passionately. He responded eagerly and made it obvious that he was ready for more, but Seraphina knew now was not the time to let him have his way with her.

Twisting herself free from his embrace, she blew him a kiss, then hurried through the rocky enclave to the place where her mare waited patiently. She allowed Harry to seat her on the animal's back and even stooped down to kiss him again. Then she dug her heels in and was away, galloping toward Witchcraven without even a backward glance at the man who stood looking so longingly after her.

The winter sun setting below the level of the hills left a deep band of scarlet in the sky, against which the ancient stones of the circle stood black and powerful. As she neared them, Seraphina reined in her horse and breathed a prayer of thanks to the all-powerful Goddess. Then she turned the animal's head and made for home.

Nearing the manor house, a gust of wind caught her hair. Tossing her head, she lifted her hand to brush it from her eyes, and there he was. Riding the ridge way that ran high above the house, his horse dark as the encroaching night, the horned man looked down on her. Seraphina gasped. Her stomach clenched as if it had been struck a great blow. Her whole body felt weak, and she had to hold hard onto her horse's rein to stop herself from falling.

He was here. What was he doing? Was he watching her? Had he been there when she and Harry had lain together? Was he guiding her, or judging her? Whichever it was, she longed for one word, one gesture from him, but he was beyond her reach. Already as she gazed longingly after him, he spurred on his horse and galloped away into the darkness.

Seraphina groaned. She bent her head forward and pressed her hand over her heart. What had she done? Up there by the stones, she had felt blessed, but one glimpse of her midnight lover and she was filled with fear and doubt. Perhaps she should have waited. There must be ways she could seek him out, find him and make him come to her. But even as the thought crossed her mind she knew that it could not - should not - be attempted; that it would be one of the greatest sins against the Goddess she could commit, one that might never be forgiven.

In which case there was no going back.

If I have made my bed, then I will lie in it, and no man will stop me, she thought, and raising her head proudly she rode into the stable yard.

The stable boy came running to help her dismount. He made to lead her mare away, but first Seraphina stroked the horse's soft velvety nose and thanked her for her patience and strength. Then, when the animal was taken to her stall to be rubbed down and fed, she went into the house.

Stepping over the threshold, she was overwhelmed by a terrible fear. What were pride and determination when set against eternal, passionate, total love? Was this what she, by ensnaring Harry, had thrown so carelessly away?

4

'Megan,' Seraphina cried as she stumbled into her chamber. 'Megan, I need you.'

Her voice shook and sounded weak, but she did not ring the bell, for she had learned long ago that she had only to speak or think of her and Megan would come. The old woman could always sense when her charge needed her. She sank down on the bed, clutching her sides.

Within minutes the door opened and Megan came bustling in. 'Whatever is it?' she cried. 'What has happened to you?'

Seraphina threw herself into the old woman's arms and burst into tears. 'I have been foolish, so very foolish. I should have waited. I should have known better. Oh, why did I do it? Why?'

'Whatever you did, it cannot be so wrong,' Megan said firmly. 'Now that you have come into your womanhood you are guided by your heart, by your deepest knowledge of yourself, as all Ladies of Witchcraven are. As your dear mother was and her mother before her. You are all led in the right ways by the Goddess herself. You have only to listen and you find and follow the path that is meant for you and you alone. So dry your tears and you will see that it is nothing, nothing of any importance.'

'But what if I didn't listen to the promptings of the Goddess in my heart? What if I went my own headstrong way? What if I have made the most terrible mistake of my life?' Seraphina moaned.

'No, no, my little one. That *cannot* be,' the old woman soothed.

'But suppose I have?' Seraphina wailed.

Megan's hold loosened. 'There is nothing you have done that cannot be put right, by the right medicine. A few herbs, a few words, a goblet of wine or two, and all will be well. So hush your crying and let Megan give you a sleeping potion to bring you happy dreams.'

Seraphina gulped down her remaining tears, then wiped her eyes on her sleeve. 'You are so good to me, Megan,' she said as the old woman helped her to undress.

The room was cold, the fire unlit, but Seraphina's crying had warmed her blood so that even the chill sheets on the bed did not bother her, and by the time Megan had returned from the pantry where she mixed her tinctures and potions, she was sat propped up against the pillows, already feeling warm and relaxed.

Valerian and poppy in an infusion of mead and honey soothed her even further, and it was not long before her eyelids began to droop. Megan took the glass from her fingers and, as she slid further into the soft embrace of the feather mattress, the old woman traced the ancient sign of blessing on the girl's forehead. Before Megan had closed the door behind her, Seraphina was sleeping peacefully.

At first her sleep was dreamless, but as the moon rose and shone its light into her chamber she began to dream.

It was high summer and, dressed only in a white shift, she was stood in the centre of the stone circle. There were flowers in her hair and twined among the belt around her waist. Their perfume rose to her nostrils, merging in with the heady scent of gorse and heather. The air was warm and filled with the sound of insects. Midges danced in the beams of the sun, which fell on the ancient stones and picked out the colours of the lichens and mosses, which in their turn softened the outline of the granite itself.

Unlike on the night of the ritual, all was peaceful and happy. Even in her sleep Seraphina smiled and stretched out her limbs in her contentment. If she could stay where she was forever she would be happy. Sitting down on the altar stone she lifted her face to the sun and, half closing her eyes, basked in its warmth. She felt it play on her face, her neck, then down over the bare skin above her breasts. Its touch was so gentle yet powerful, it begged her to give herself up to pure, simple enjoyment.

Seraphina sighed with pleasure.

'My lady, I see, worships the sun as well as the moon.'

The voice in her ear was deep, yet soft. The whisper of breath against her neck made her pulses stir. Leaning back, she felt the heat of the body behind her. Hands rested on her shoulders and pulled her closer. She leaned against him, breathed in his scent of sex and the wild wind and a deeper musky smell that was his alone.

'You have come to me,' she murmured.

He did not reply. His lips were busy, moving over the back of her neck. Soft and gentle, barely touching the skin, yet making every nerve tingle with desire. His hands moved lower, his fingers cupped around her breasts, then teased the nipples through the thin material of her shift.

Under his touch, the twinges of pleasure she felt grew into waves. She wanted his hands to move downwards, his fingers to touch and stroke the lips of her labia, to find their way into the dark moistness of her vagina. But oddly enough there was no urgency to any of this. She could wait. He would take his time and she would savour every quivering sensation. They had all the time in the world to enjoy. Her legs fell open, her buttocks contracted, and in spite of her resolution to take her time, her hips began to move.

'My lady,' he murmured.

He slid his hand between her legs and she shuddered as his fingertips teased over her. Pressing herself back against him, she was about to give way to her orgasm when she realised that he was in fact lifting her so that she was on all fours. Once she was in position, his hands moved to her buttocks. His fingers massaged them, kneading the firm flesh as she quivered with anticipation.

'Time,' he murmured. 'We have all the time we might wish.' And suddenly she knew this was true. This was no climax she must race to ride, this was pleasure to be taken slowly, and savoured.

Breathing in, she closed her eyes, focused on every move he was making. His hands cupped her bottom and he rose above her, his cock brushing against her, touching the quickening lips of her vagina. Lifting her head, she opened herself up to him, but he withdrew. She gave a little yelp of frustrated desire.

'Patience,' he breathed. And he was there again, hard and firm, banging against her gaping, pulsing entry, before moving away. Seraphina drew in her breath and tightened her muscles so that when he made another run at her, she was taut and firm, resisting rather than submitting.

'So that's the way of it.' Through the quickening breath, the scent of his passion, there was laughter in his voice.

'It is indeed,' she managed to gasp. But then he was inside her, thrusting his way to her pleasure, coming in great spurts as she screamed and shuddered and climaxed not once, but multiple times

Finally, completely satisfied, glowing, sleepy, yet bubbling with joy, she turned to face him. For a moment he was standing above her, and although in her dream she could not see his face, she knew by some joyous instinct that he smiled. Smiling in return, she stretched out her arms. She wanted to hold him, to kiss him a light butterfly tease of a kiss. A thank you for the game they had played, so light-hearted and yet with feeling. But before she could even touch him, he was gone.

Her feeling of happiness however remained. She woke with a feeling of deep contentment, bathed in its golden glow, a smile on her lips.

A thin winter sun flooded through the greenish glass of the ancient windowpanes. It made no impression on the icy chill of the room but, still warmed by her dreams, Seraphina did not care that her breath rose into the cold air. She pulled the covers up to her chin, her knees up to her chest, and smiled as she let herself remember every part of her dream in vivid detail.

Her midnight lover was skilled and knew exactly what to do to please her. Was it because the horned man was not only human, but part god? She shook her head. The man who had pleasured her in the Goddess's midnight ritual at the stones that first night was as real as she was. The masks the worshippers wore gave them mystery and power, but beneath them these were men and women she might meet in her daily life, not sacred beings descended from the heavens.

If he were not a god, then was he merely something she had imagined, a perfect lover to fill her dreams? Seraphina shook her head and laughed out loud. Not only had she breathed in his scent, his musky perfume and the smell of the wild wind, but with her lack of experience she never could have imagined the way in which he had taken her, nor - and here the laughter died away as she came to the heart of the matter - nor could she have dreamed the light-hearted joy of their coming together. Yet there was feeling and passion there too. So what was it?

In her frustration she banged her fist against her knee. And with the blow came the answer. What had happened on the altar stone in her dream was two people in tune with each other, a man and a woman in whose union was a perfect balance of power. In their play neither was dominant. Unlike with Harry, where she orchestrated every move, while making sure that he thought he was in control of her, she and the horned man had no need of such games. If they chose to be playful, it was their mutual choice; if they chose to rut in a frenzy of passion, they were both free to do so. Whatever they did, it was with the other's total consent. He was not dominant, neither was she. They were – Seraphina gasped at the outrageous idea – perfect partners.

Was this what the Goddess wanted of her? And of him? She lay back on her pillows and wondered, if that were true, how she could make it happen.

The door opened and Megan bustled in.

'You slept well, my little one.' It was a statement, not

a question, for the old woman knew only too well the power of the herbs and the strength of the enchantment she had used to make Seraphina's sleeping potion.

'Oh yes,' Megan,' Seraphina cried.

'Your dreams were good. I can see that by the flush of your cheek and the sparkle of your eye,' the old woman grinned.

'Beyond good. They were magnificent, amazing! Words fail me to describe where I have been and what I have done this night. All I can say is, may the Goddess be truly thanked for where she led us.'

'Blessed be She forever,' Megan said, bowing her head.

'Blessed indeed,' Seraphina echoed. Then, clapping her hands and throwing off the covers, she declared that her dreams had given her such an appetite that if she were not fed that very minute she would fall to devouring the bedposts to stave off her hunger.

'What, and break your teeth on that ancient wood? Surely not, for no man, whether in your dreams or not, would look at a toothless crone,' Megan shrieked with laughter.

'Then hurry and help me dress, or I will not be able to help myself!'

Baring her teeth, Seraphina lurched toward the bed, then collapsed on the mattress in a fit of giggles.

'Well that will get you nowhere,' Megan chided, pretending to be cross.

Still laughing, Seraphina let the old woman lace her into her corset and petticoats, then slip over her head a scarlet dress of the finest wool.

'There's ice on the windows and frost on the ground. We would not want you taking a chill, not after the heat of your night,' the old woman said firmly when

Seraphina pulled a face at the plainness of the garment. 'And wrap a shawl about your shoulders,' she added. 'The fire in the parlour has only just been lit, and it's as cold as a tomb in there this morning.'

I hate being so poor. Why is it that we must scrimp and save on every little thing? Seraphina thought crossly as she ran down the stairs to the dining parlour. *When I am Harry's wife, and mistress of Hamer Hall, then I shall have a fire in every room, whether we use it or not.*

Hand on the doorknob, she stopped, her heart leaping to her throat as she realised what she had been thinking. If she married her cousin Harry, as she fully intended to do, then she would never, ever achieve that perfect union she had experienced in her dream. Her midnight lover would never take flesh. He would become nothing but a fantasy, something to be conjured up when she tired of her husband. As she surely would. As all Ladies of Witchcraven did. For the men they chose were the men who would give them the daughters to carry on the line, to perform the scared rituals of the Goddess at the stone circle. It might be that they had been loved once, loved and desired, but when the child had been conceived and safely brought into the world, then they had no further use for their husbands.

Seraphina ground her teeth and clenched her fists. Even though what she felt for Harry would not last, she was determined to have him, if only to show her father that she, unlike any ordinary woman, was not his possession, but had a will and mind of her own.

Besides, she comforted herself with the thought, once she had her daughter then she could take a lover, or two. And maybe, though she hardly dared hope it, among them there would be the horned man. Except, with a deep sigh, she realised that that would never happen.

The lover of her dreams would never share her with anyone, nor would she share him. If she ever found him again, then they would be bound together for all time.

A pitiful fire hissed and spluttered in the hearth. A jug of spiced ale stood beside it, and there was bread, and a platter of cheese and slices of meat set out on the table. Seraphina held her mug in her hands and stood as close to the fire as she could. The hot drink warmed her and she was about to start on her food when the door was flung open and her father stamped in, bringing with him the heavy smell of horse, sweat and wine.

Sir Greville's cheeks were flushed from his ride, his hair was wild and his clothes crusted with mud and stained with wine and food. Without greeting or even looking at his daughter, he went straight to the ale jug and poured himself a tankard. When this was gone, he filled it up and drank again, then wiped the few remaining drops from his chin, before letting out a huge belch.

'Food,' he roared. 'What a man needs after the night I've had is sustenance. A roast leg of lamb, a joint of beef, not this pauper's fare.' He lurched toward the table, and for a moment it looked as if he was going to sweep all the dishes and plates onto the floor – an action Seraphina, who was still hungry, was not going to tolerate.

'Good morning, Father,' she said coolly, and there was something in her voice that brought him to his senses, for his arm dropped, he stumbled up against the table and, holding onto the edge, turned his bleary eyes on her.

'Good day, daughter,' he growled. Then, glancing wildly at the fare in front of him, he seized a hunk of bread and stuffed it in his mouth. Chewing with his lips wide open, he gulped, swallowed, then looked around for something to wash his mouthful down.

Seraphina got up, poured him another tankard of ale and handed it to him as demurely and sweetly as a dutiful daughter should. Her action seemed to trigger something in her father, whose face cleared. With some effort, he focused his eyes on her and grinned wildly.

'You're a good girl, a good, good girl,' he muttered.

'I should hope so, sir.' Seraphina decided to keep up her role of obedient offspring.

'You are, you are,' her father continued. He raised a great red paw and reached over to pat her arm.

Seraphina drew in her breath and forced herself to sit still as he mauled and stroked. How her mother could have stood to have him anywhere near her, she could not imagine. All she could think was that her father must have been very different in those dim, distant days when the Lady of Witchcraven chose him as the father of her child. She looked at the drink-sodden face, the body gone to fat, and for a moment wondered if the same would happen to Harry once he had fulfilled his function in her life. No, it would not, she decided. She could never bear to keep as pathetic a creature as this near her. Harry would remain Harry, or … She shook her head quickly to cast out the thought before it even took shape. Megan had potions that could cut short the life of any living being, even one that had not yet been born. Besides, Harry and she would be happy. She had decided, and it would be so. With this thought in mind, she managed to smile at her father.

'Good girl,' he muttered, as if she were a dog, or a bitch that had pleased him in some way. 'Yes that's what you are.' He nodded happily. 'A good girl, who deserves good things. Who will be dressed in silks and satins, will ride the finest horses, drink the finest wines, eat the best food that gold can buy. You, my Seraphina, my angel child, will be rich and happy, and it will be all thanks to your dear father, your kind and caring father, who has thought of nothing but your good since the day you were born.'

Oh yes?, Seraphina thought, knowing full well from what Megan had told her that her father had been disappointed by the birth of a daughter and had spent the rest of his marriage to her mother hoping for a son and heir.

'When I marry my cousin Harry, then I will be rich and happy,' she said softly. There was no harm in seeding the message in his mind, so that soon, very soon, he would think that the union of the cousins was his own inspired idea.

'Harry?' To her surprise her father's head came up and his forehead furrowed into a deep frown. 'Who said anything about you marrying your cousin?'

A flush of anger stained his face, and Seraphina, who wanted to avoid a repeat of the previous day's outburst, hurried to say, in as soothing a voice as she could manage, 'I must have misunderstood.'

'Yes you did. You certainly did. No daughter of mine is ever going to wed that miserable milksop of a nephew. I'd not lower myself, nor you neither, to stoop to such a thing. So let that tight-arsed sister of mine, with her prick of a husband, put that in her pipe and smoke it!'

The image of Lady Harriet smoking a pipe was so funny that Seraphina had to put her hand up to her mouth to hide the smile that she knew would infuriate her father even further.

'No. As I told you yesterday, I have arranged a much better match for you.'

'Yesterday?' The smile fled from Seraphina's lips.

'Yes. I told you. God's britches, do you never listen?'

I listen, but you rarely speak sense, Seraphina thought. 'I told you, sir, did I not, that I would marry a man of my own choosing,' she said.

'*A man of my own choosing*,' Sir Greville mocked. 'Never. No child of mine will marry whom she chooses.' He bunched his hand into a fist and thumped the table so hard that the dishes rattled. 'You are mine. Under the law, everything you have and are belongs to me. What I say goes, and you have no choice.' Each of these last words was punctuated by a thump of the fist.

Seraphina clenched her hands beneath the table and forced herself to keep calm. Her father could shout and bluster all he liked; in the end, her will would prevail. However long she might have to wait, she would do as she wished and have the man she wanted.

'Lord Brandon is a good match,' Sir Greville stated. 'For God's sake, you can have no objection to a man of his wealth and standing in the county. Any other girl would give her eyeteeth to have a husband such as he. Any other girl would be on her knees in gratitude to her father for finding her such a husband. But not you,' Sir Greville ended bitterly. 'God'strewth, what did I do to deserve such an ungrateful bitch of a child.'

The same thing I did to deserve such an unfeeling brute of a father, no doubt, Seraphina thought acidly. Her father's news was not what she had expected. She had thought his bluster about a good match had been no more than wishful thinking on his part.

'Lord Brandon is a fine man,' he insisted. 'He'll keep you satisfied and fill you with sons. And he's rich. One of the wealthiest men in the kingdom, so they say.'

'Then what will he want with me? A poor man's

daughter with little but the manor for my dowry,' Seraphina flashed.

Sir Greville looked at her and his face clouded. He frowned heavily, his thick black brows meeting over the bridge of his nose, his eyes murky with incomprehension, until the answer to her question struck him.

'He'll take you. Any man would take you, if,' he paused, 'if you wanted him.'

'What if I do not want him?'

'Be reasonable,' Sir Greville wheedled. 'Lord Brandon is better than that half-grown schoolboy you fancy. I have no doubt my sister's husband has other plans for him. Besides which, they're a long-lived family, so you'd have to wait for your fortune. You know we need the money. Witchcraven bleeds the stuff from me. The land is poor. The tenants won't pay their rents. I've had nothing but trouble with the estate, small as it is, since your mother died.'

That's because you haven't cared for it as you should, Seraphina thought, but she said nothing, and her father continued:

'Lord Brandon has the money now, and he's handsome, or so they tell me. Marriage to him will solve all our problems.'

'I'll not lose Witchcraven,' Seraphina cried.

'I'll not ask you to. You're more than welcome to the damn place. Brandon has agreed that he'll take it as your dowry.'

'Never. No man shall have Witchcraven. It is in my mother's will. These lands must be passed from daughter to daughter. If you dare to break the terms, you will be cursed forever, your flesh will rot from your bones, your ...'

'Enough! Hold your tongue, you insolent hussy.' Sir Greville raised his hand and caught his daughter a stinging blow across her face. Seraphina staggered and would have fallen if she had not managed to grasp hold of the back of a chair. 'You'll marry him, and if you don't, I'll flay the skin from your backside and keep you in chains until you do.'

Seraphina put her hand to her cheek. Her head spun and she was so angry she would have cursed her father on the spot, if she had thought that it would make any difference. Sir Greville was a slow thinker, and it took him a long time to come a decision about anything that did not involve the breeding of a horse or a dog, but his daughter knew that once he was set on a course of action, it was impossible to deflect him. Many were the cold, lonely hours she had spent as a small girl locked in the cellar until she had agreed to do what her father told her. If only, she sighed inwardly, she could find her midnight lover. He would rescue her from this impossible situation. But that was not to be; so, assuming the mask of a dutiful daughter, she lowered her eyes and, swallowing her pride, managed to nod her head.

'That's more like it.' Her father puffed out his chest. 'That's what I want to see. You won't regret it, my girl. Not when you're the mistress of Brandon Hall, with all the servants at your beck and call. Then you'll see how well your dear old father has looked after you. I've arranged for his lordship to call this afternoon, so treat him well and show him what a bargain he's getting in my little filly.'

Sir Greville made to pinch her cheek, but Seraphina moved swiftly away and he had to content himself with a swift pat on the bottom.

Maybe the old goat is not as stupid as he appears,

Seraphina mused as her father left the room. *He senses my power, but on the other hand he will not let me use it. There must be some way out of this situation. I cannot marry Lord Brandon. I must choose my own husband, as all Ladies of Witchcraven have done over the centuries. I only wish it could truly be the one man in all the world I desire as my eternal soul mate.*

Seraphina sighed and, leaning her elbows on the table, stared out of the ice-rimmed window.

'What is it? What ails my nursling? After such a night of dreams there should be nothing for you to sigh over,' Megan said when she came into the room to clear away the breakfast dishes.

'It's Sir Greville.' Seraphina stuck out her lower lip. 'My father has taken it into his thick head to arrange my marriage, and I am not sure how I am to prevent it. He says it is the only way we can save Witchcraven. But I do not believe him.' She stroked her still-glowing cheek. 'There must be some other way. Oh, Megan, you will help me find it, and at the same time put a stop to this unwanted marriage, won't you?'

The old woman ignored her question. 'Who is to be the happy husband of the happy bride?'

'Oh, that doesn't matter,' Seraphina said impatiently. 'What matters is that unlike every other girl I make my own choice.'

'Who is he?' Megan persisted.

'Why do you have to know?' Seraphina stamped her foot. Megan gave her a warning glance, and instead of flying into a tantrum, she said, 'My father has decided on Lord Brandon as a fit mate for his only daughter.'

'Lord Brandon,' Megan considered. 'You could do worse. A great deal worse.'

'But I don't want him. I want to marry my cousin

Harry. As you well know. As you have always wished.'

'Harry is a fine lad, but Lord Brandon, now there would be a catch for you, my little one.'

'A catch!' Seraphina's voice rose. 'What do I care what society might say about my marriage? All I want is the man of my choice. I want someone young and strong and lusty who will bed me and give me a daughter so that the line of the Ladies of Witchcraven will remain unbroken for another generation. Oh, Megan, surely you can see that is all that matters to me? Lord Brandon may be rich and handsome, but so is Harry. At least, he is not rich yet, but he will be. Besides, he is the one I have fixed my heart upon, and that is that.'

'You mean to say that Harry is your heart's desire?' Megan gave her another of her soul-piercing looks, and for a moment Seraphina found it hard to hold the old woman's gaze. But she was determined that no-one, not even her beloved nurse, should ever know who it was that reigned in her heart – for to admit that she was in thrall to her mysterious lover would make her seem weak. So she kept her eyes fixed, and it was Megan who was the first to look away.

It was the first time Seraphina had ever bested the old woman, and although a small corner of her heart felt a pang of regret, she was nevertheless swept by an amazing sense of power and triumph.

'So you will help me avoid this marriage,' she said – and it was a statement, not a question.

'I will do what I can, my lady,' Megan said. 'But even the Ladies of Witchcraven must act with caution. You cannot defy your father outright. Sir Greville has the power of life and death over you, and if he wished, he could beat you senseless and throw you out into the street.'

'If that happened, there would be plenty of people who would take me in and care for me.'

'That is true, but you would lose your heritage. You would lose Witchcraven and all that goes with being its Lady.'

'Never. No-one can ever take it from me.'

'That we do not know. The power of the Lady of Witchcraven is bound up with the place, or so it has been since time immemorial,' Megan said slowly.

Seraphina had to admit that what the old woman said was probably true. If Sir Greville disowned her and threw her out, the followers of the Goddess would make sure that she did not starve and had a roof over her head. They could not however defy the law of the land, nor would she want them to. If she wanted to keep the manor and hand it down to her daughter and her daughter's daughter then she would at least have to appear to do what her father wanted.

'If I do what my father wants, then what about Harry? I as good as promised myself to him,' she said at last.

'Oh, young master Harry,' Megan twisted her lip. 'There's no need to worry about him. You can do whatever you please with him. If I know you, my lady, and I do, you have him for life, or at least for as long as you want. So use him at your pleasure. As for the other one, Lord Brandon ... We will have to see what we can do.'

5

When Megan had bustled away, Seraphina sat staring out of the window for a while longer. Out there was the ancient stone circle, and somewhere out beyond that was the one man she wanted more than any other in this world. He however was unobtainable; Harry and now apparently Lord Brandon were not.

Her thoughts lingered over the last time she had seen her cousin, and in spite of her anger at her father and her sense of frustration about her position, she smiled. It had been so easy to seduce him, easier still to make him believe that it had been all his idea, and that he had been the one who took the lead, whereas in reality she had orchestrated every move.

It was good to be in control. Seraphina's hand strayed to her breast, the other fell to her lap. She opened her legs slightly, wriggled her bottom on the seat of her chair, moistened her lips with her tongue. She was growing damp, the scent of her musk rose around her, it would take only a moment …

With a brisk, decisive move Seraphina pushed back her chair and sat up. This was no time to pleasure herself. Swishing her skirts, she hurried up the stairs to her bedchamber. There she found paper, pen and ink and, kneeling at the window seat, she wrote:

My Darling
    All is lost. My father has arranged for me to marry Lord Brandon. Come to me. My heart is broken.
    Yours forever, your despairing cousin,
    Seraphina.

Holding the letter up to the light, she re-read it and smiled a little grimly. This should bring Harry running to her side, and it was possible that it would stir him into action. Perhaps he would fling her over the back of his horse and ride off with her to some distant parish where they could be married. Or whisk her away abroad, returning only when their families had both consented to their marriage.

No. Seraphina shook her head and laughed a little bitterly. If anyone was to suggest such desperate remedies it would be her, and much though she wanted to defy her father and do what she wanted, somewhere deep down inside her she knew that she would not; she could not risk losing Witchcraven for any man. Except one.

Seraphina pinched her arms viciously. From now on she must forget about him. If she was to succeed in her plans then it must be as if he did not exist, or at the very least was no more than a passionate dream.

She sealed the note with a blob of scarlet wax and then, throwing her cloak around her shoulders, made her way to the stable yard.

Frost made the cobbles slippery, and the horses' breath rose warm and sweetly scented into the still air.

Seraphina took time to stroke her mare, to whisper in her ear and lay her head against her strong neck. She wished she could saddle her and ride away over the moors, but it was not to be. It was growing close to midday. In the afternoon Lord Brandon would call, and she had not yet decided how to greet him. Would she do as her father had commanded and put on a fine dress and act the lady, or would she stay as she was? By now her dress would smell of the stable yard, her hair was wild and still uncombed, and she could, when pushed, do a fair imitation of the local accent, which would make her seem slow and uncouth. Not the sort of girl a man of means and breeding would want as his wife.

'My lady, would you like me to saddle the mare for you?' Almost as if she had conjured him up, the stable boy appeared at her side.

'I wish I could ride this morning,' Seraphina sighed, and let the faintest trace of a tear sparkle in her green eyes. 'But I cannot. My father, Sir Greville, has said I must stay at home this afternoon. I do however have a very urgent note I must send.' She paused.

'Then let me, my lady. Let me take it for you,' the boy cried eagerly.

Seraphina frowned a little and appeared to consider. 'It is all the way to Hamer Hall,' she said doubtfully.

'Oh, that is no distance at all, my lady,' the boy replied cheerfully. 'I'll take old Betsy – she's in need of some exercise – and I'll be there and back in no time at all.'

'Be sure to wait for a reply, won't you?' Seraphina said.

'I will,' the boy assured her. 'I'd do anything in the world for you, my lady,' he murmured under his breath.

Seraphina knew she was not supposed to hear him,

but her ears were sharp, and she had to suppress her smile as she thanked the boy and urged him to hurry on his errand as fast as he could go, because she would not be able to rest until she had the reply to her note.

What would Harry say? What would he do? Would he surprise her? The thoughts beat endlessly in her head until Megan asked her if she had ants in her stockings, she was so restless.

'I've sent a note to Harry,' Seraphina said.

'Why in the Goddess's name would you do that?' Megan cried in exasperation.

'I thought – oh, I don't know what I thought,' Seraphina cried, furious with herself for telling her nurse. 'I am so … I do not know what.'

'You need a strong man, that's what you need.' Megan tapped the side of her nose and winked. 'The sooner you are bedded by a lusty husband the better you will be. It is your time to be wed and there is no fighting it. Forget Harry. He will never be able to give you what you need. Go with this new husband, this man your father has found for you. Sir Greville may not be what he once was, but he knows how to breed true. Just you look at his horses and his dogs. Men come from all over the county and beyond to have an animal of his breeding, and if he has none to sell, then they come for his advice as to which stallion to put to which mare and which dog to mate with their prize bitch. He'll have studied the bloodlines of your new husband and his ancestors as far back as possible, and you could do well to do as he says.'

Seraphina pulled a mutinous face, but she had to agree that there was some sense in what Megan was saying.

'And don't frown,' Megan scolded. 'Young or old, rich or poor, no man likes a woman with a face like crumpled linen.' Then the nurse's expression cleared. 'That is, unless she has other parts ripe and ready for the offering,' she cackled. 'Now let me bring you some hot water to wash in, and I'll brush your hair until it is so sleek and silky that your Lord Brandon won't be able to keep his hands off your tresses. Oh, we'll make him hot and ready for you, don't you worry. By the time I've finished with you, he'll be wanting to strip you bare and have you then and there on the hearth rug.'

'In front of my father?'

'Well, maybe not that hot for you,' Megan grinned. 'But primed enough.'

'That's as maybe, but I told you, I don't want him,' Seraphina pouted. 'Oh, Megan, you said you would do what you could, and now all you want is to make him lust after me. I'd rather he were indifferent, that he took one look at me and decided I'm not worth it. After all, I'm poor, and though I come from an ancient family, it's not considered one of the best.'

'Humph,' Megan blew down her nose. 'Your line stretches back to the Goddess herself, so don't you go saying anything different, my girl. You don't want to offend the Lady by your words.'

'Of course not,' Seraphina cried. 'Oh, Goddess forgive me.' She bowed her head and prayed that her idle words would not bring bad luck on her head.

'That's better. Show you're sorry and give yourself up to Her will. Remember, if She wants this marriage, it will take place. If, however, She wants you to mate with your cousin Harry, that too will happen. All you have to do is listen to your heart and obey.'

'I know,' Seraphina murmured, softly digging her nails into her palms to drive away the rebellious image of herself spread-eagled on the altar stone, the horned man thrusting into her with such vigour that the whole of her body pulsed and vibrated with unalloyed pleasure.

The colour rose to her cheeks, her breathing quickened and she had to turn away from Megan and move over to the chest where her dresses were kept to try to conceal her arousal. 'If I have to meet with Lord Brandon, what shall I wear?' she asked as casually as she could manage.

'A dress would be best. You'll not meet him in your shift, not yet,' Megan cackled.

Seraphina bit her lip to suppress her impatient sigh. 'Which dress?' she said.

Megan bustled over to her side and lifted the lid of the chest. A scent of lavender and cedar rose into the air. 'Scarlet, emerald, or white? Red as fire, green as your eyes, or pure as a lily?' the old woman muttered over and over again as if chanting the words of a spell. Finally having made up her mind, she lifted out a green silk dress. 'This one, I think. It brings out the colour of your eyes. It is as fresh and young as the spring.'

'To show my innocence and youth,' Seraphina took up the game.

'As light as a whisper.' Megan held up the silk and let it swing gently in the air.

'To show how light-hearted and easy-to-please I can be.' Seraphina seized the dress and twirled it about as if she were dancing with a partner. 'Except I am neither light-hearted nor easy-to-please, and I will not have him think so.'

Flinging the garment down on the bed, she strode over to the chest and slammed down the lid. 'I shall wear what I have on my back. He shall see me for what I am. A poor girl with a love of riding and the countryside I may be, but I will not pretend to be anything else for any man. What he shall see will be what he shall get.' *Except he shall not see what lies beneath the surface. The power I have from the Goddess will blind him, because I wish it to. If at any time I wish to change this, then and only then will I reveal my true self to him.*

'Sir Greville will not be pleased,' Megan muttered.

'What do I care!' Seraphina tossed her head. 'As far as I'm concerned, my father can go to the devil for his part in this, and the sooner the better.'

'Tut, tut,' Megan clicked her tongue. 'You do not mean that, my lady. It is your temper not your sense speaking. You will care, if he beats you for your bad behaviour.'

'Just let him try,' Seraphina growled, even though she knew that if her father did give vent to his anger she would have no way of stopping him.

'Whatever has got into you this morning?' Megan scolded. 'Whatever it is, you must guard against it when Lord Brandon comes to call. Now sit there, by the fire, until I come with the hot water, and then at least I can be sure that you will have a clean face and hands for your visitor.'

What imp has got into me? Seraphina wondered as she sat by the miserable remains of the fire and stared at the guttering flames. *I really am not myself today.* She knotted her fingers and twisted her hands. *It must have been the dream that has so upset me. It showed me what I can never have, and now my father and Megan between them have shown me what I must settle for. But even if I have to go along with their plans, they will not have it all their way.*

Megan came back with a bowl of steaming water scented with lavender. She dipped a muslin cloth into the water and sponged Seraphina's hands and face, then dried them carefully and rubbed in a rich cream of her own making. It had a powerful scent that hung in the air and masked the smell of the stable yard. Then she began to brush and comb Seraphina's hair, pinning it up on the top of her head, except for one long lock that she pulled free and let fall over the girl's shoulder, so that that it fell tantalisingly over one breast.

'He won't be able to keep his eyes off it. He'll itch to move it just a little, to follow its lead below your bodice,' she murmured.

'No!' Seraphina leapt to her feet so violently that she almost knocked the old woman to the ground. With a toss of her head, she flung the lock back and fastened it firmly behind one ear. She checked in the mirror, but the effect did not please her. 'Put it up,' she demanded. 'Scrape my hair back from my face. No enticing wisps or curls. Make it as plain as a Quaker's on her way to meeting, if you please; and if you don't I shall do it myself.'

To her surprise Megan did not protest. The hair was quickly fixed, and a plain black ribbon was fastened round Seraphina's neck in place of the silver locket the old nurse had suggested.

'Show me,' Seraphina demanded when she was ready. Megan held up the mirror to her, and she twisted and turned to try to get a glimpse of herself in the pitted glass. At last she was satisfied that she looked as plain and ordinary as she could make herself. Taking up a piece of sewing that she had no intention of ever completing, she went downstairs into the parlour to wait.

The time seemed to drag forever, but at least it was warm. In honour of their visitor, or at least to stop his blood from freezing in his veins, Sir Greville had had the fire banked high, and the logs crackled and spat in the hearth as the flames leapt up the chimney. Her father sat to one side of the fire, dressed in his best coat and clean britches, with his favourite spaniel, Floss, at his feet. He stretched out his feet, leaned back in his chair, and soon his eyes closed, his mouth fell open and he began to snore.

On the other side of the fireplace, Seraphina basked in the unfamiliar warmth and wondered how long she too would manage to keep awake. Her eyelids were drooping, her limbs relaxing. The sewing slipped from her fingers and she could feel herself slipping into sleep.

Suddenly there came a sharp yelp from Floss, and the animal sprang to its feet. Sir Greville's head jerked back. The spaniel started to bark furiously and, joined by the other dogs that had lain in various places round the room, rushed to the door.

'God's britches, he's here!' Sir Greville hoisted himself to his feet. 'Come along, girl, no sulkiness now, show his lordship your best face. Remember the future of Witchcraven depends on how you behave toward our visitor.'

If it didn't, I'd kick him where it hurt and run off with Harry, Seraphina thought, smoothing down her skirts and lifting her chin. 'I shall be the perfect lady, never you fear,' she said, so smoothly that her father, smelling a rat, glowered warningly at her; but before he could say anything, the door opened.

The man that stood in the doorway was tall and handsome. His shoulders were broad, his waist narrow. Dressed in black silk, with falls of the finest lace at his throat and cuffs, his hair tied back behind his neck, Lord Brandon strode into the room as if he was already the master of Witchcraven and all within.

'My dear fellow,' Sir Greville beamed. 'How good of you to come.' He held out a fat, beefy hand, thumping his visitor on his back as the men shook.

Seraphina, watching him closely, thought his lordship winced at this familiarity; but if he did, it was a fleeting thing, and his expression as he approached her was masterful, dominant. He clearly expected her to give way, to flutter her eyelashes, to blush becomingly. Seraphina smiled inwardly. If that was what he wanted then he would have to whistle for it.

'My daughter, Seraphina.' Her father lumbered up to her and beamed at them both.

'My lady.' Brandon inclined his head in a brief bow.

'My lord.' Seraphina imitated the gesture. She wondered if she was expected to curtsy. She knew she should stretch out her hand for him to kiss, but instead she set her lips in a polite smile and waited.

Lord Brandon raised an eyebrow and shot her a quizzical look as if to say, *Whatever you do or do not do next, I can take it in my stride.*

'She's a good girl. Fit, healthy, a looker too.' Her father sounded as if he were selling a mare, not introducing a daughter to her suitor.

'Mistress Seraphina is indeed beautiful,' Lord Brandon said politely.

'Thank you, my lord,' Seraphina said blandly. She tried to look over his shoulder as she spoke, but there was an energy about him that forced her eyes to meet his. His searing glance drained her will. Drawn by his almost irresistible magnetism, she took a step toward him. Her breath quickened, her legs felt as if they would not hold her for much longer.

But Seraphina was not going to give in. She bit her lip. Drawing herself up to her full height, she saw that Lord

Brandon was neither annoyed nor overawed by the way she had refused to act the part of the soon-to-be blushing bride. Far from it. Judging by the slight upward curve of his lip, he was in fact laughing at her. Her temper bubbled. Here she was, refusing to be either intimidated or charmed by this admittedly handsome and dashing man, and he found the whole situation amusing! How dare he! Seraphina lifted her chin, half closed her eyes and shot him a look of the most utter disdain.

'You'll not find her any trouble,' Sir Greville went on. 'A firm hand is all she needs. Keep her on a short rein and beat her when she annoys you.'

Seraphina bristled, but before she could say anything, Lord Brandon spoke:

'I am sure beating will not be necessary, unless of course the lady desires it.' His voice was deep and husky, his glance questioning.

The thought of his hand on her sent tremors of desire coursing through Seraphina's veins. She realised that it was a desire he shared. He wanted her. That must be why he had approached her father. Sir Greville would never have dared to offer his daughter to someone so wealthy and well-thought-of. He knew only too well how most of the county viewed their shabby hand-to-mouth existence. Most of the time he did not care, so Lord Brandon must have been very persuasive – which proved beyond doubt that he wanted her, and what was more, he wanted her enough to marry her. Seraphina smiled; she could not help herself. If Lord Brandon wanted her, then she knew just how to play him. Suddenly the whole tangled situation in which she found herself became totally manageable. Megan had been right all along. If her father insisted, she would marry this man, but to show her independence, she would keep Harry as her lover. What was more, she and she alone would choose when his lordship would have her; and if it did not suit her to give way to his desires on her wedding night, then she would not.

'I am very glad to hear that you will give your wife the respect due to her,' she said coolly. And confident that this time he would not draw her in, she looked him straight in the eye.

'I give every woman the respect she deserves.' Lord Brandon's voice was equally cool. 'As you will learn when you become my wife.'

'I was not aware that the matter had been settled between us,' Seraphina said, turning away from him.

'Your father and I have agreed. You are to be my wife, and since there is no legal or moral impediment to our marriage, we will be wed before the next full moon.'

'There may be no legal or moral impediment, but it is usual to seek the consent of the bride,' Seraphina said.

'Any other woman, it is true, I would woo. You, my lady, strike me as one that prefers to come straight to the point. We are to be wed. You are to be mine.'

He moved toward her, seized her arm and, pulling her roughly to him, kissed her. The moment he touched her, every nerve in her body tingled with desire. She was moist, she was hot, her heart was pounding, her nipples were straining at her bodice. His lips were hard on hers, his tongue probing. Melting in his arms, she could not help herself. For a long, delicious moment she clung to him, gave herself up to his strength, opened her lips to his, drank in his taste. Her eyes closed, her hips thrust toward his groin. Swooning, she sensed his hardness; then, as suddenly and abruptly as he had seized her, he flung her away.

'Remember you are mine,' he said coldly. 'Greville,

my lawyer will call on yours. Let the settlement, such as it is, be drawn up and the wedding prepared. A fortnight and I will make her Lady Brandon.' And without another glance in her direction, he was gone.

'There's a man who knows how to treat a woman,' Sir Greville sighed with satisfaction. 'Mean and hard, that's the way to keep them in their place. Take that look off your face, my girl. You enjoyed it, I could tell. I can always tell when a bitch takes pleasure in the act, and you're made for it, like your mother was before you. Out of the same stable, the pair of you. If only she had not been taken so young.'

His eyes filled with sudden tears and, half blinded, he staggered toward the sideboard, where he poured himself a large brandy. Gulping down the drink, he wiped his eyes on his sleeve and sniffed loudly.

'A proud woman like you needs a proud man. You'll be happy with him. You'll bless the day I made this match. Mark my words, you will.'

'Never!' Seraphina cried. She was not going to give in, even though she suspected her father was right. 'I despise him and I always will. A man who cannot give his wife-to-be a civil word is not fit to be in the same room as her. He is a boor, an animal, and I will never, ever, ever love him.'

'That's it, that's my girl. You'll be singing a different tune on your wedding night.'

Restored to good humour by the brandy, her father slapped her bottom as she swept past him, and his laughter echoed down the corridor as she stormed out of the room and fled to her bedchamber.

Flinging herself down on her bed, she beat the pillow with her fists and kicked furiously at the mattress, until finally, her anger spent, she turned over on her back and, staring up at the faded canopy, began to plan her revenge. Poison was her first thought: something deadly to rid herself of this arrogant lordship forever. Hands behind her head, she stretched out comfortably as she contemplated the most painful potion Megan could concoct. But to watch him retch and groan would give her no pleasure. It would be no better than poisoning a rat; and, unlikely though it was, there was always the possibility of discovery – which, Seraphina shuddered to think, would mean a public hanging for her and for her old nurse. Poison therefore was not the answer. She wanted something that would prick his damned pride, something that would show him he was not the irresistible lover he obviously considered himself to be. Lord Brandon might think that any woman he turned his not inconsiderable charm upon would be willing to fall instantly on her back and offer herself to him, but she, Seraphina de Lacy, would show him how wrong he was. If he wanted her, he would have to change. She would school him as her father schooled an evil-tempered horse, and she would begin on their wedding night. 'By the Goddess, that will be revenge indeed.' Seraphina sat up and stretched out her arms in a gesture of triumph.

A knock on her door wiped the smile from her face. As a rule, no-one knocked on her door and waited. Megan, sure of her welcome, would come straight in, and the servants would tap quickly as a warning and do the same. Surely it could not be Sir Greville come to gloat over the success of his plan? Seraphina frowned. Her father's satisfaction was not something she wished to see, although it was, she had to admit, most unlikely to be him. For one thing, he would surely barge in without a by-your-leave, and for another, now that he had what he wanted, he was far more likely to turn his attention back to his dogs and his horses. The knock came again.

'Come in,' she called.

The door opened a crack and a boy's face appeared.

'Right in,' she insisted. 'Don't lurk in corridors.'

'No, my lady, I'm sorry.'

It was the stable boy. Twisting his cap in his hands, and with his face flushing bright red, he said, 'I hope I did right.'

For a moment she was puzzled, then he continued:

'I had to wait and wait, but at last they brought the message out to me, and I rode back as quick as old Betsy could bring me. For I remembered that you said you would not be able to rest until you had your reply, and I could not bear the thought, indeed I could not, of you fretting and worrying for so long.'

'Yes, yes. Give me the note,' Seraphina said impatiently. Then, as the boy's face fell, she added in a softer, more enticing tone,' You have done well, very well. You have spared me a great deal of unease. For that I must thank you.'

'Oh, my lady.' The boy looked as if he had been transported to paradise.

'Now run along.'

The boy gave an awkward little bow and was moving toward the door, still staring at her adoringly, when Seraphina changed her mind.

'No, stay. Let me read my letter first.'

She scanned the note hastily, frowning as she read.

'Is all well?' the boy asked anxiously.

'As well as can be,' Seraphina replied with a smile. 'You can saddle my horse, for I wish to ride. Go on – what are you waiting for?'

The boy glanced out of the window at the gathering dusk. 'Nothing, my lady, but it's getting dark, and …'

'Of course. You, unlike others, have a care for my safety. But you do not need to concern yourself. I have changed my mind. I shall not ride tonight.'

The boy's face registered his relief, and he went off happy.

When he had gone, Seraphina lit a candle stub from the ashes in the hearth and looked over what Harry had written:

My Dearest Love,

Say only the word and I shall swoop down on Witchcraven and carry you away. We will go to some far-distant place where prying eyes will not find us, and live out our love forever. As soon as you get this, come to our special place.

Your devoted lover,

Harry Fitzgerald.

'Hmm. He'll meet me at our special place. That is all well and good, but it will be dark by the time I can get there, and I do not wish to find myself out on the uplands at night without a lantern to guide me. Harry will have to wait.'

She put down the note, then instantly picked it up again. She could not leave Harry waiting out there on a cold winter's night. It would truly put his love for her to the test, and she did not want anything to sway his complete and utter devotion to her, not if she was going to wreak her revenge on Lord Brandon. How was she going to get a message to him? She had sent the boy back to the stables, and although she could send for him again, or go down and see him, she did not want him to know of either her secret place or her tryst with her cousin. The only person she could trust with such an errand was Megan, but Megan was too old, too slow. Besides, Megan was in favour of her marriage to Lord Brandon, and it was quite possible that the old woman would simply refuse to do her bidding. She was not at Seraphina's beck and call like the rest of the servants. Since Megan had brought her up from babyhood, she was very firm about what her self-willed young charge should and should not do. On the other hand, Seraphina was no longer a child. Since the ritual at the stones, her powers were growing. She was well and truly the Lady of Witchcraven, and as such Megan should do her bidding.

Seraphina slapped her forehead with the palm of her hand. Of course, that was the answer. She had no need of messengers. She would summon Harry to her. It was true she had never attempted any such thing before, but that was when she was still being taught about the powers the Goddess gave her followers.

Seraphina went to her window. Kneeling on the window seat, she rested her elbows on the sill and gazed out at the darkening landscape. Up there on the hill above the house stood the stone circle. A little distance from it was the jagged cleft in the ground where she and Harry had taken their pleasure of each other.

She had led Harry into its deep and private shadows. She had kissed and caressed him. Lifting his hand to her lips, she had covered it with the lightest, softest kisses before drawing his longest finger into her mouth and sucking it, letting it slide in and out, in and out, until unable to bear it any longer, he had thrust his cock against her thigh. Sinking down, unbuttoning his straining britches, marvelling aloud at the length and width of his member, she had taken it into her mouth, lapping and licking until she had tasted the first salty drop of his come, when she had leapt to her feet and, drawing him deeper into the darkness, had spread her skirts, opened her legs and let him thrust into her eager, pulsing cunt.

Seraphina moaned softly. The mere thought of his cock made her wet and hot. She let her hand trail down her leg, pressing it hard against her mound. The cry came again to her lips, her hips moved forward, she pressed herself against the coldness of the wall. Through the glass she saw the moon low over the uplands, pictured Harry with cock rampant and erect, and slid her hand under her petticoats.

Goddess, she was so soft, so warm, so wet. Her fingers stroked the rough hair. She wanted to wait, to conjure him to her, but she could not. Her labia were wide, her juices hot and musky. Even if she went no further, even if she resisted the firm hardness of her finger, she would come. Seraphina did not hold back. As her fingers touched her clitoris, her orgasm swept over her. Her body pulsed, her hips thrust and she cried out, remembering only at the last moment to use his name.

'Harry, come to me. Come as I am coming!'

When her trembling had subsided, when she glowed with warmth and basked in the scent of her coming, her finger wet with her musk, she traced his name on the steamy surface of the windowpane. Then she rearranged her skirts, wrapped a shawl around her shoulder and waited.

It did not take long. Even before the chill of the room had made her skin prickle with goose bumps, she sensed he was approaching. Taking her cloak, she slipped out of the house. Instead of going into the stable yard she made her way round the side of the house toward the orchard.

Pushing open the wicket gate, she stood on the

threshold of the walled enclosure. Like everything else at Witchcraven, this too had been neglected by Sir Greville, making it a perfect place for children to play out of the gaze and care of adults, if they did not have time to sneak up to the hidden cleft in the uplands.

Seraphina hugged herself under the coarse folds of her cloak. Where better to meet on a cold winter night, when everyone else would be huddled close to the fire? The walls would afford some protection from the frost, and no-one would ever think of looking for her in this desolate part of the manor.

The moon lit the gnarled shapes of the unpruned fruit trees. Long shadows fell between the rows and she picked her way carefully until she came to the furthest wall. Here she stood in the shelter of the rough brick and, clenching her fists hard against her thighs, shut her eyes and began to empty her thoughts, until she saw nothing but the figure she began to form in her mind. A handsome, fair-haired young man with an open face and a ready smile.

His arm slid round her waist, and for a moment she thought it was the strength of her need and her imagining. She opened her eyes and he was there, pulling her close, his lips desperately seeking hers. Her arms twisted round his neck and she pressed herself against his solid warmth.

'Harry,' she murmured. 'Oh, my Harry.' His hair flopped over his forehead and she reached up to push it away.

'I cannot lose you,' he groaned. 'I must not. Come with me now. Run away with me.'

Seraphina swallowed. Held so close, knowing that he would always care for her in the same determined way that he did everything, she was almost tempted to do as he said. Surely a cottage in the wilderness with loyal, easily-managed Harry was better than the fight she would have bringing Lord Brandon to heel? But even as she leaned into him, as he showered her hair, her neck, her breasts with kisses, she knew that Harry was ale to his lordship's champagne; that life with her cousin, however dear he was to her, would quickly stale, while with his lordship it would remain a constant challenge to the end.

If she married Harry, he would eventually become another Sir Greville, despised and considered good for nothing but the everyday running of the estate. At least with his upbringing he would manage her lands better than her father. But even though he might rescue Witchcraven and bring it back to the honour and prosperity the estate had once enjoyed, she could not do this to her cousin. Seraphina knew herself. She knew her desires and her fiercely independent temper. Harry was too soft, too pliable for her. He was, however, exactly what she needed at that very moment.

Wiping her eyes as if they had been filled with tears, she looked up at him and murmured, 'Where would we go, if we ran away together?'

'To London, or Paris, or maybe Italy. I would love to show you Rome and Florence. Anywhere so long as we can be together for the rest of our lives.'

'I wish,' she sighed. 'But how will we live?'

'I have my allowance from my father, and one day I will inherit Hamer Hall.'

'And in the meantime we will find some hidden cottage where we will live on love and fresh air?'

'If that is what you want, then that is what we'll do. Only come away with me, let me wrap you in my cloak, set you on my saddle bows and ride away into the dawn with you cradled in my arms!' Harry cried passionately.

'No, I cannot. I cannot do this to you. You are your father's son. Running away with me would break his heart. He would disown you, and me too,' she added softly, bowing her head so that he had to lean down his to catch her last words. 'We would live our lives in poverty and misery, and in the end you would blame me for your misfortune and I would blame you.'

'Never. Seraph, you are my angel. I could never blame you for anything. Besides, this is my idea. It is what I want more than anything in the world.'

'It may be now, while we are both young and strong. While I am still young and you desire me. But beauty, strength and desire, they all pass away, and then what would we have left?'

'Each other,' Harry persisted stolidly.

If only … Seraphina thought for a wild moment. *If only I was not bound blood and soul to Witchcraven. If only I had not been chosen as the Lady. If I had not undergone the ritual of the stones. Then, oh then, I might well have taken you at your word, settled for the everydayness of your love. Been your wife and had your children.*

'Oh, Harry.' She reached up and stroked his cheek. 'For those words alone I could love you.'

'I mean them. So come away with me, Seraph. Stop this and come. I have gold in my pocket and credit in London.'

'I cannot.' Surprised at her own reluctance, she freed herself from his grasp.

'I love you. If you will not come away with me now, then refuse this marriage. Tell your father you will not marry Lord Brandon. Throw yourself on his mercy. You have only to wait for me and I will lay my fortune at your feet.'

'Your father is hale and hearty and we must not wish him ill,' Seraphina said almost primly. 'Besides, you know my father. He is as stubborn and immoveable as the hills. Once he has made up his mind, then there is no swaying him. Marry Lord Brandon I must.'

Harry clamped his hand over her mouth. 'I cannot bear even to hear you speak of it. He shall not have you. I'll kill him first.' His eyes gleamed furiously in the moonlight.

'No!' Terrified he might do something stupid, Seraphina grabbed at his arm. 'No, you must not. You are too precious to me. Promise you will do nothing so stupid.' She kissed him passionately, and when at last she paused for breath she repeated, 'Promise me Harry. Swear on my life.'

'I swear,' he said reluctantly.

'Good,' she murmured. 'I will keep you to that vow.'

'Or else?' he said miserably.

'Or else I shall put an evil spell on you.'

'You'll turn me into a toad?' Entering her game, he half grinned.

'Oh no. I shall do something far worse. I shall ...' Her eyes opened wide and green. 'I shall ...' Her hand reached down between his legs, her fingers began to undo his buttons. 'I shall turn this noble gentleman ...' She dropped on her knees and, taking his freed cock into her mouth, sucked gently, before moving her head back and continuing, 'I shall turn his majesty into mush, so that ...' Her lips went to work again. 'So that he will never ...' She withdrew. 'Ever ...' She sucked more strongly now ... 'Pleasure any woman ever again.' Licking out her tongue, she lapped him, pulling with her lips, drawing him in and out of her mouth until he was on the verge of emptying himself into her.

'Seraph!' he groaned.

'Harry!'

His hands were in her hair, twisting, pulling, his hips ground toward her, and with a yell he came. His shudders echoed through her body. In spite of her resolution that this was to be his night, she felt herself respond. With the taste of his come still in her mouth, she got to her feet, pressed herself against him, guided his hand down between her petticoats to the throbbing little knob that protruded through her open labia. She wanted him to kiss her there, to lick her into orgasm, but she was already coming, in short, sharp bursts of pleasure that left her smiling as she kissed him on the lips.

'Is this it, then?' Harry asked miserably as she stepped out of his embrace. 'Now you're engaged to that damned Brandon fellow, will I never see you again? Will we never do this again?' His voice broke and he looked so downcast that Seraphina had to bite back her laughter.

'Of course not. This is but a foretaste of how things will be between us. You will always be my dear cousin and my dearest lover; at least until one of us changes our mind.'

'That won't be me. Never,' Harry declared.

Seraphina shook her head. 'Who knows? Who knows what the future may hold? In the meantime, we will have to be careful – at least at first.'

She kissed him lightly again, and he would have pulled her back against him if she had not sidestepped quickly.

'Tell me,' she said, partly to distract him, partly to assure herself. 'How did you know where to come tonight?'

'You sent a boy with a note. I read it and saddled my

horse and came as soon as I got it.'

'I sent a note saying we were to meet in our special place on the uplands,' Seraphina said.

Harry grinned and shook his head. 'Seraph, the shock of your father's decision has addled your wits. The note said as plain as plain we were to meet in the orchard at Witchcraven. Here, I'll show you.' He rummaged in the pocket of his coat. 'No, damn it, I won't. The blessed thing seems to have lost itself. Oh, now I remember. I burnt it in case anyone saw it and knew where we were going. If I still had it, you would see that you had told me to come here. There was no doubt about it. Even before I had mounted Captain I knew where I was heading.'

'And so you always will. You will come to me when I need you,' Seraphina cried delightedly. 'See, all is not lost.' And with a quick wave of her hand she hurried away into the darkness of the moon shadows.

6

'You will wear your white silk for your wedding,' Megan said.

'What? Am I to display my virginal purity to all and sundry?' Seraphina said sulkily.

'You will wear white because white is the colour your mother wore and her mother before her. White is the colour of the moon and of the Goddess herself when she is maiden.'

'And scarlet is her colour when she is at her ripest,' Seraphina said. 'Or should I wear the black of mourning?'

'Not on your wedding day. You are no crone.'

'I feel like one.' Seraphina kicked moodily at her chair.

It was a chill cold day. The sky was grey, the light that filtered in through the thick panes of her chamber dim and dismal. The clouds threatened snow, which did not fall, and a miserable thin wind whined around the house. It shook the shutters and sneaked in through every nook and cranny, chilling her blood, so that however close she stood to the fire she simply could not get warm.

'I am frozen to the very bone. I am sure my feet are sprouting chilblains, my nose is red. I look a perfect fright, and you want me to wear my white silk in two days' time. I shall die of the cold, I know it.'

'Whatever has got into you? You have done nothing but moan these past few days. What you need, my girl, is a strong, lusty lover to warm your blood and shut your mouth, and thank the Goddess you will not have much longer to wait for one.'

'Two days,' Seraphina muttered. 'In two days' time I will be Lady Brandon.' She pursed her mouth and would have spat if Megan had not shot her a warning glance. Instead she pulled a face and, swishing her skirts, stamped about the room.

'Goddess save us. If you are in such a bad way, do you not know how to scratch your itch?' Megan sighed and raised her eyes to the roof.

'I can do that well enough,' Seraphina grinned, in a sudden swing of mood. 'I do not choose to do so. Megan, do you not think it rather rude and uncouth of my soon-to-be husband to pay me no attention since his last visit, which was,' she stopped and pretended to count the days, which she knew only too well, 'fifteen days ago, I think?'

'You think right. But why are you surprised? From what you told me, you sent him off with a flea in his ear, and no man, however noble and rich, likes a woman who treats him as you did.'

'No man who is worth his salt would put up with such treatment, that is sure. Oh, Megan, I fear that this Lord Brandon, who has such a high opinion of himself and his charm, is nothing but a limp rag. One less-than-loving word and he runs off in a sulk to lick his wounds. What I am going to do with such a pathetic creature, I hardly dare think. If you wonder why I feel like a bitch in heat with a large dose of fleas, that is why. I told you,' Seraphina whirled round and faced her old nurse. 'I told you, didn't I, that I should marry my cousin Harry. He would never have treated me like this.'

'Your cousin, my lady, also appears to have run off. We've seen neither sight nor sound of him either since your betrothal.'

'That is because my father has forbidden him to come to the house before the wedding,' Seraphina said loftily, 'not because he fears what I might say or do. Harry loves me. I know it. And ...' she paused.

'You do not love him,' Megan said briskly. 'So stop your moping and come over here and try on your dress while there is still time to make any alterations.' The old woman screwed up her eyes and looked the girl over from head to toe, then clicked her tongue in disapproval. 'I do believe you may have lost a little weight. That is not good. A bride must not lose her looks. You should be plump and buxom as a young heifer ready for the bull.'

'Moo.' Seraphina giggled, and Megan's face creased into laughter. 'Are you saying, my dear nurse, that I am nothing but a cow?'

'I am not, indeed. Though if you were a little more like one, you might be happier.'

'Shall I chew the cud then and fart worse than my father?' Seraphina laughed. 'Will this do?'

Making as rude a noise as she could manage, she put her arm around her nurse's waist and whirled her round in a wild dance. Round and round the room they went, until her head spun and the old woman begged to be released.

As suddenly as it had come, Seraphina's good humour deserted her. She slowed her dance and, careful not to hurt Megan, helped her onto a chair, where she sat with her head in her hands, moaning softly.

'I am sorry,' said Seraphina. 'I am truly. Oh, I am such a bad girl.' She knelt beside her nurse and put her head in her lap.

Megan's chest heaved and wheezed, and for a terrible moment Seraphina thought she had gone too far, but gradually the old woman's breathing became more regular and she put her hand on the girl's hair and stroked the wild tresses gently.

Tears sprang to Seraphina's eyes. 'Oh, Megan, how will I manage without you?' she wept. 'Can you not come with me? I will tell my father that I must have you, that I will pine away if I do not have you to care for me.'

'There, there, my little one. You will not be that far away. Brandon Hall is nothing but a short ride for you. You know Sir Greville will never agree that I should come with you, nor will Lord Brandon if he is anything like they say. He will want everything grand for his new wife. He'll not put up with a crooked old woman who, never mind how much she loves you, is nothing like a pretty young ladies' maid.'

'You're not an old crone – or at least you may be, for the Goddess has blessed you with Her wisdom and skill. You are like a mother or a grandmother to me, and I need you!' Seraphina cried passionately.

It was true that she had never been without Megan in all her life, but there was another reason why she wanted to keep her old nurse close. Megan worshipped the Goddess and had taught Seraphina all that she knew; but still Seraphina suspected there was more the old woman had to tell. Also there was her skill with herbs and tinctures. There was no ailment that Megan could not treat. She could mix a potion to bring down a fever, to soothe aches and pains, whether of the body or the soul. She could use her deep and ancient knowledge to bring on sleep, or something deeper.

All this remained unspoken, although Seraphina suspected that Megan knew what she was thinking, but still the old woman shook her head and clicked her tongue as she had done when Seraphina was little and had begged and begged for an extra sweetmeat.

'No man wants his wife's mother or grandmother living in the same house as them. No matter how much the young wife might beg, it would be a weak man to give way, and Lord Brandon is not one of those.'

Megan chuckled, and Seraphina had a quick image of his lordship's fine figure, his broad shoulders, his narrow waist and hips, the firm roundness of his buttocks. She felt the fire rise to her cheeks and hastily looked away, not wanting Megan to see her reaction.

'Besides, I cannot leave Witchcraven,' the old woman went on. 'My place is here. What would I be in some grand house?'

Seraphina sighed and nodded. Megan was right. Somewhere like Brandon Hall she would be no more than one of the servants, not the power she was at Witchcraven, where everyone treated her with the respect she deserved.

'You can come and visit whenever you like, I'm certain of that,' the old woman continued. 'And in due time, when Sir Greville has gone to his rest, then you will have Witchcraven all to yourself.'

'That might be years yet. I cannot bear it. I cannot bear leaving this place. It is where I was born, where I belong. What is Witchcraven without its mistress?'

'Never fear, you will not be away from Witchcraven for long,' Megan soothed.

'How do you know? What if my vile beast of a husband insists I stay at Brandon Hall with him?'

'I know because I have seen it,' Megan said simply. 'When you told me what your father had in mind for you, I was worried and afraid. Then I told myself that these things are meant to be. I prayed to the Goddess, and then I scried.'

'And you saw me here? You saw me back at Witchcraven?'

'I did, my little one.'

Seraphina sighed in relief and sat back on her heels, her eyes intent on the old woman's face.

'And his jumped-up lordship, was he with me?'

Megan's face clouded. Her eyes grew filmy, her mouth slack, and when at last she spoke, her voice sounded faint and troubled.

'That, my little one, I did not see. I poured the water again and again. I made the offerings, but nothing came. I saw you, here where you should be, but of him,' Megan shook her head and sighed, 'there was nothing.'

'Good.' Serphina got to her feet. 'That must mean he no longer trod the Earth. An early death. It is no more than he deserves.'

'My lady, never say such things, even in jest,' Megan protested.

'You are right, of course.' Seraphina hastily made the sign of protection. For if the Goddess heard her idle words, what might She do? Besides, on reflection, death was not what she wished for his lordship – not, that is, until she had broken him to her will, and that could be done only while he was alive and full of lust.

If only he would come to her. This absence on his part was not right. As her betrothed, he should visit her every day to pay her court and ripen her up for their wedding night. What did he think she was? A whore who would open her legs to any man who paid for her favours? Did he think that her father had sold her to the first man who would take her without a dowry? Or did he sense that she was a woman accomplished in the arts of love, who could pleasure him in ways he had not yet imagined? If she willed it.

If she was right, then she would soon have him in her power. Seraphina smiled lazily as she thought of one or two of the things she might do to his lordship. It was, all in all, better to be a whore than a virgin for her plan to succeed. Though even a whore could do with some courting.

The thought had scarcely crossed her mind when Edwith, one of the village girls who helped in the house and kitchen, came bursting in.

'Oh, Mistress Seraphina, the messenger said to bring it straight to you. It was not to stay in my hands for longer than a breath, for they are none too clean, nor fine enough for this.' She thrust a fine leather pouch into Seraphina's hands. 'He did say, too, I was not to wait and see, but to hurry back to my tasks as quick as flight. So there you are, miss.'

Edwith bobbed a curtsy and fled.

Seraphina felt the weight of the pouch, let her fingers linger over the Brandon crest embossed in the soft leather.

'Well, go on, open it,' Megan said, her eyes gleaming with anticipation. 'It's a jewel, no doubt about it. Sent by that husband-to-be of yours as a wedding gift. Now, what do you say about that?'

'Nothing. It still comes too late,' Seraphina replied haughtily. She was not going to show her nurse what she really felt. She was at once annoyed by the lateness of the gift, intrigued by what it could be and fired up by the challenge it represented. From what she knew, and more than that from what she intuited, this gift was the next move in their battle for dominance.

'A family piece, you mark my words,' Megan babbled happily. 'A necklace, by the look of it, that you are to wear on your wedding day. And if I know anything, it will be finer than any piece your poor dear mother ever had.'

'I would rather wear her locket, with her portrait and the lock of her hair, between my breasts on my wedding day, than any piece of Brandon jewellery,' Seraphina said coldly. But her heart was beating fast as she slid the jewel case from the pouch.

The case was made of deep blue leather, the colour of the night sky before it darkens to blackness, and on its lid was emblazoned the Brandon coat of arms in sliver, bright as a new star.

'Go on, then,' Megan prompted as Seraphina hesitated.

Catching her lip with her teeth, Seraphina lifted the lid. On pure white velvet, untouched as virgin snow, lay a silver necklace. The metal was tooled and shaped and set with moonstones, milky white with a flash of blue like drops of water. At the centre was a single larger stone set between two leaping silver hares. The total effect was both barbaric and beautiful. It was something no lady would ever wear, and at the same time it was perfect for her. How did he know? Her fingers were drawn to the jewel, and she longed to see it round her neck, hanging just where she wanted it on the voluptuous curve of her breast, suggesting both the delights to be had and the purity of the woman who wore it.

'Both virgin and whore,' Seraphina breathed. A perfectly chosen present from a man who knew what she was; who, without even having her, had plumbed her depths, both of body and spirit. And this was the man she had sworn to herself she would master.

Suddenly the room swam around her head. Seraphina put out a hand to save herself from falling. She clutched at the bedpost, leaning against it until at last the dizziness passed and she could open her eyes, to see Megan's face creased with anxiety.

'You sit yourself down. Come on now.' The old woman's arm was around her waist, lowering her gently onto the lumpy mattress of the old bed. 'There now. Keep still and it will pass.' Lowering her voice, she mumbled words that Seraphina could not catch, but that calmed the panic in her blood and soothed her breathing. 'Better now?' Megan smiled.

'Much better,' Seraphina agreed.

'I'll fetch you a potion, then. You'll not be wanting to be fainting and swooning on your wedding day,' Megan said.

'I'll not be fainting or swooning, you may be sure of that,' Seraphina said firmly.

'You won't indeed, not after my medicine,' Megan assured her. 'Stay still and do not move. I will not be long.'

Seraphina waited until Megan had shut the door behind her, before jumping to her feet. The jewel case had fallen from her grasp when she became dizzy, but the necklace had been held fast inside it, and Megan, once she had tended to her, had put both case and pouch carefully on the windowsill.

'As if offering it to the moon,' Seraphina thought, then angrily shook her head. This must stop. She'd not be intimidated by this gift. She would shut it up in the chest with the rest of her wedding clothes and make up her mind later whether or not she would wear it on the day. In the meantime she would not think of it, nor what it might mean.

As she walked over to the window, however, she caught sight of a piece of paper lying on the floor. Picking it up, she saw her name written on the thick parchment. Like the jewel case, it too was sealed with the Brandon crest, and for a moment she was tempted to fling the whole thing out of the window, or to set fire to it on the hearth. In the end, however, she decided that she needed to know what insulting message he had sent with his gift.

Slitting it open, she read, 'To my Lady of the Moon. Eternally, G.'

Seraphina gasped. The note slid from her nerveless fingers. How did he, how could he, know that the Goddess was linked so closely to the moon? Or was it no more than a lucky guess?

She took a deep breath and made herself look at the note again. For one wild moment she hoped that it might be from someone else. Who, after all, was G? Then she remembered that Lord Brandon's first name was George, and her heart began beating wildly again.

Who was this man who had taken her on so suddenly and unexpectedly? And what did he really want from her? A cold shiver slid up her spine. Could it be that it was not her, but Witchcraven itself he desired? If it was, then she would die rather than let him have her beloved manor.

Crumpling up the note, she flung it to the back of the fire, where it would burn once the fire was set. She slid the jewel case into the pouch and threw it into the chest.

'Diamonds; you should have sent me diamonds,' she hissed as the lid clanged shut. 'That's what a proper man, a real gentleman, would have done,' she added. But her voice shook at the thought of Brandon's strangeness, and her blood beat wildly as she wondered what this would mean for her.

7

On the eve of her wedding, Seraphina dreamed of the stone circle. A full moon hung low over the ancient site. Long shadows reached out toward its centre, where she stood on the altar. Her face was hidden beneath a bird mask. The feathers reached out over her head, making a fantastic crown above the tumble of her dark curls. A heavy silver torque hung around her neck, her breasts were bare and she wore a pleated kilt around her hips, fastened with a wide silver belt set with moonstones and amethysts. Silver bands circled her wrists and in one hand she held a whip.

Lifting the whip high, so that the leather gleamed like a snake in the moonlight, she held it above the back of the man who knelt on the ground at her feet.

'Goddess of the moon and stars, Maiden, Mother, Crone, yours is the punishment I exact on this pitiful human,' the words came unbidden to her lips. She cracked the whip and brought it down hard on the naked back of the kneeling man. 'For what you have done, for what you deserve,' she cried again, and once more the lash tore at his skin, until the blood ran and he cried out in pain. 'Do you acknowledge your fault? Do you admit your sin?' Seraphina demanded.

The man at her feet raised his head. It was Lord Brandon. 'I am yours, and I submit myself to your will, now and always,' he said.

Filled with an almost unbearable joy, she brought the whip down once more over his shoulders. Then, stepping down from the altar stone, she took his hand and raised him to his feet. Like her, he wore nothing but a pleated kilt, and through the fine linen she saw his arousal. In one swift movement she pulled the garment from his hips. His cock stood proud and hard. Seraphina stretched out her hand and ran one long white finger down his shaft. Unable to help himself, he groaned, and she instantly withdrew.

'Silence. You are to remain silent and still until I give you permission,' she hissed.

His hips moved, he bit down to suppress his cry, but she would give him no mercy. A quick flick of the whip across his naked buttocks left him quivering for more. Seeing his need, this time she slid her hand down his member, reached down to cup his balls, before releasing him. In the moonlight she could see the bead on his tip. With the arousal of her senses she could smell the briny scent of his juice. But it was not yet time. He would have to wait, trembling, subservient, until she was ready to give him what he wanted.

'Oh, my lord, you have insulted one favoured by the Goddess,' she murmured, moving so close to him that her nipples brushed his chest, her hips moved toward his. 'For this you must bear your punishment,' she whispered, close up to him now, her arms winding around his neck.

His cock pulsed against her belly. She had only to lift herself up onto the altar stone then slide her hot, wet self over him, let him reach deep into her inner depths; but it was too soon. Ready though she was, she must make him wait.

'Are you ready to beg for Her forgiveness, to give yourself utterly to Her will?'

'I am,' he said.

'Then take your place on the altar,' Seraphina cried. 'On your back, and not a word, not a sound, or it will be the last you ever make.'

She took the knife from her belt and held it up to the moon. His eyes, dark and unreadable, watched her every move. Seraphina's lips moved, chanting strange, mysterious words she had never heard before. Her body began to sway and the knife in her hand glinted, the muscles of her arm forcing it downwards. He did not flinch. She saw the flash of fear in his eyes, sensed his sudden tensing as the weapon skimmed his flesh, but it did not diminish his arousal; if anything he grew harder, bigger, as with one wild cry she pushed aside her skirts and mounted him. One hand over his mouth she rode him, writhing and twisting every grain of pleasure from him until her climax rose to such pitch that the stars and planets spun around her, she was lifted to another sphere of pleasure, and gripping him hard with her thighs she came. Almost immediately he joined her, his back arching, his hips thrusting as he was carried along with her wild ecstasy.

She did not stop to touch him; there was no caress, no kiss. Rising from the prone body on the altar stone, she smoothed down her skirt and strode out of the stone circle without a backward glance.

Her mare was waiting for her at the edge of the circle, placidly grazing the short green grass. Seraphina swung herself onto the animal's back and rode away down the narrow track to Witchcraven.

She woke with a smile on her face. A fire flickered in the hearth, filling the room with an unaccustomed warmth and the air with the sweet scent of applewood and pine cones. A towel had been hung to warm over the back of a chair. A hip-bath of steaming water was placed beside the fire, and Megan stood beside the bed holding a pewter tray.

'Happy dreams?' Megan grinned.

'The best.' Seraphina stretched and yawned triumphantly. 'If this is an omen for my marriage, I shall be a very happy bride indeed.'

'The Goddess gives what the Goddess wills,' Megan said.

'Whatever that might mean,' Seraphina replied carelessly.

'Here, eat and drink. You will need your strength for later.' The old woman plumped up the thin pillows and handed Seraphina a goblet of spiced wine.

Seraphina sipped the hot drink, enjoying the way it slid through her blood, leaving her warm and relaxed. Then she nibbled at sweet bread, thick with dried fruits and laced with honey that reminded her of long lazy afternoons in the herb garden where the bees buzzed around the lavender bushes.

'That was good,' she murmured, licking the last of the sweetness from her fingers. Beneath its honeyed taste she detected another sharper, saltier flavour, which brought back the full glory of her dream. Or was it a dream? Given the tang of him on her skin, could she be sure that the scene enacted on the altar was purely one she had imagined?

'Megan?' she began, then stopped. Dream or reality, what did it matter? It had given her the strength to keep to her resolution. Besides, whether it had happened or not, if the old woman did not want to tell her then she would not. Maybe there was a reason for her silence. Or maybe the Goddess had spoken to Seraphina alone, and Megan knew nothing.

'It's a fine, bright day for a wedding.' Megan walked over to the window. 'There's a sharp frost and a sprinkling of snow as fine as stardust. Not that you should be wed at this time of year. The Lady of Witchcraven should take her man at Midsummer Eve, but it will do, it will …' She stopped. Her hand rose to her mouth. She drew in her breath. 'Oh,' she gasped. 'Oh, my lady.'

'Whatever is it?' Seraphina threw back her covers and, leaping out of bed, joined the old woman at the window. She did not however simply peer through the thick glass, but flung open the casement and, leaning out into the frosty air, gazed in wonder at the creature on the edge of the hill. Like some steed from legend, the stallion was as white as the snow that dusted the hillside. Noble as the finest horse her father had ever bred, his coat shone in the morning light, his bridle gleamed sliver and the deep blue of an evening sky. With a proud gesture, he tossed his head, before rearing up on his hind legs as if to take possession of all he surveyed. Then, to Seraphina's surprise, instead of galloping away over the uplands, he flicked his tail and, taking the steep downward path, trotted toward Witchcraven.

'My lady,' Megan cried, as Seraphina flung a cloak over her nightdress, thrust her feet into a pair of slippers and raced down the stairs and out into the clear, bright morning.

A clear blue sky arched overhead, and Seraphina's breath rose into the air as she watched the magnificent stallion approach the manor house. As he neared her he slowed, stopped and bowed his head in complete submission to the Lady of Witchcraven.

'Moonlight. You are Moonlight,' Seraphina breathed, and the horse, acknowledging his name, gazed deep into her eyes. She stroked his mane and buried her face in his neck as he nuzzled her shoulder and she breathed in the scent of his breath. They stood there, horse and woman, oblivious to everything else around them, until the spell was broken by an elf-like groom wearing the Brandon livery.

'His Lordship hopes his wedding present will please his lady. He says to tell you he has sent Moonlight for his moon lady,' the man said.

Seraphina's hand dropped from the stallion's neck.

'His lordship, Lord Brandon, told you to tell me this?'

'He did, my lady.'

There was a twinkle in the groom's eye; a wild woodland gleam that suggested he knew more about his master's gift than he was telling.

'Send him my thanks. Tell him his gift is …' Seraphina hesitated. Lord Bandon's gift was perfect, but it was also disturbing. With its references to the moon, it hinted at a knowledge of her, of who she was and the powers she possessed, that he could not possibly have.

Moonlight whickered softly as if he too was worried.

'It's all right,' she whispered in the animal's ear; but even as she murmured these reassuring words, her stomach tightened. She gritted her teeth. The gift of the stallion, however magical, was not going to change her mind, or her attitude, toward the giver. Lord Brandon was not going to win her over with presents. She had to remember her dream. The Goddess had sent it to show her the way. She was the dominant one, not he. As

Moonlight had bowed before her in complete submission, so would his master.

She gave the horse a final pat. Aware now of the icy cobbles beneath her feet, her skin prickling with the cold, she called the head groom to find the stallion a stall.

'Oh, and send the stable boy to me in the kitchen,' she said as the man led Moonlight toward the stable yard. 'At once, man. I cannot wait any longer in this bitter morning.'

In spite of its thick walls, the house was little warmer than the yard. Seraphina wrapped her cloak around herself, but the damp struck up from the stone flags and cold draughts slid in through the cracks and crannies as she waited in the corridor that led to the kitchen. The boy had to come this way from the stables, and she wanted as few people as possible to see her talking to him.

Leaning back against the wall, she kept her cloak around her so that she merged into the shadows, and when he came running into the house, eager to do his mistress's bidding, he did not at first see her.

'My lady, I …' he stammered as, silent as a ghost, she stepped out in front of him. 'You sent for me?' His face flamed scarlet, and Seraphina had to hide her smile at his embarrassment.

'I have a message I want you to take,' she said, so softly that the boy had to move closer, which made him blush even harder.

'Of course, my lady. Anything for you. I'd do anything, go anywhere …'

'I know,' Seraphina cut him short. There was no time if she wanted to put her plan into place. The boy held out his hand, but she shook her head. 'There is nothing written. You must see Mister Harry and tell him yourself.'

'Tell him what?' The boy's forehead creased with anxiety, and for a moment Seraphina wondered if she was making a mistake choosing him as her messenger. But who else could she send? These days, Megan rarely left the grounds of the manor. Besides, it would take the old woman too long to get to Hamer Hall and back, and if she went, who would help her get ready for the wedding? The other servants were busy with the preparations, and her father's groom she did not trust, while this boy had already proved himself reliable.

Beckoning him even closer, she murmured, 'Tell Mister Harry and him alone, you understand?' Then she bent her head and whispered in his ear, 'All is set for tonight. We act as planned.'

'We act as planned,' the boy mouthed the words silently to himself, and Seraphina nodded and smiled.

'Exactly,' she said. 'Now hurry. Go and return as swiftly as you can. Make sure that no-one sees you or notices you are missing. If they do, then say I sent you to …' She hesitated for a moment to think of a convincing reason. While she searched her brain, the boy said:

'To fetch you some lucky heather from the hillside, my lady?'

'Perfect!' Seraphina clapped her hands and he beamed with pleasure. 'Now go, as quick as the wind and as silent as the mist.' She placed her hand on his head as a sort of blessing, then he was off as fast and as silent as she could have desired.

When Seraphina returned to her room, she found Megan waiting for her. 'You smell of the stables,' said the old woman, wrinkling up her nose and pouring more hot water into the hip-bath.

'No wonder, because that is where I have been.' Seraphina shrugged off her cloak, slid out of her nightdress and lowered herself into the scented water. The steam rose around her, she smelled the perfumes of summer flowers, and with a sigh of pleasure she let the water lap over her.

'Running around like this on your wedding day,' Megan clicked her tongue in mock disapproval.

'I had to see the gift my soon-to-be lord and master had sent,' Seraphina said.

'And a very fine one too, I've no doubt.'

'Moonlight is the most wonderful horse I have ever seen. I doubt my father himself has bred such a fine specimen. But Megan.' Seraphina sat bolt upright as the thought occurred to her. 'How did he know?'

'Know what?' The old woman moistened a rag and began to wash the girl's back.

'That I would call him Moonlight. That the moon in all her phases has a special meaning for me.'

'All women are linked to the moon and its tides,' Megan said.

'I know that.' Seraphina shook her head impatiently. 'But that is not what he meant by his gift. A woman's ties to the moon and her cycles are not something men think about. Her ties to the Goddess, however …' She stopped and turned her head, trying to catch the old woman's eye. Had Megan let something slip? Or had her nurse come right out with it and told his lordship about the connection between the Lady of Witchcraven and the worship at the stone circle?

'I said nothing. You know how it is and how it must be,' Megan said severely, showing yet again how she could read the girl's thoughts. The look she gave her made Seraphina feel guilty.

'I am sorry. I know that you would never betray us. But however hard I rack my brains, I cannot think how he knew.'

'He loves and wants you. Love is powerful,' Megan said, pouring hot water over Seraphina's hair and rubbing it with her specially milled soap that left her curls thick and glossy. Seraphina blinked and shook the water from her eyes.

'I still neither love him nor want him,' she said, but even as she spoke, she knew she was lying. She did not love him, that was true, but as for wanting him … A faint cry came to her lips as she remembered the wild hardness of his kiss.

'And there is the necklace, the moonstone,' she continued, working herself up into a fury against him, 'when it should have been diamonds, or sapphires, or emeralds. What kind of a man gives his wife stones such as these? He is a man who is rich enough to buy up the whole county, if he wished, and all he can spare me are those paltry stones.' She glared at the chest into which she had thrown the jewel box.

'Lord Brandon is a man who knows what he has taken on,' Megan said slowly. 'Where would my Lady of Witchcraven be with jewels such as those?'

'Rubbish. He knows me not at all,' Seraphina said, a little too loudly, to quell the uneasy feeling at the pit of her stomach. 'He wants my body, he wants to show me who is master; but Megan, I am more than equal to him.' With a spray of water, she rose to her feet like a goddess rising from the waves, her breasts firm and taut, nipples erect, stomach rounded, limbs white in their perfection.

'Have you prepared what I asked for?' she asked as her old nurse wrapped a warm towel around her.

'Aye, my little one,' Megan murmured. 'It will be ready in your chamber when you want it. I shall bring it myself so there will be no mistake. Now sit yourself down there on the stool by the fire and let me dry your hair.'

'This is how it was when I was little,' Seraphina said with a catch in her voice. 'Oh, Megan, how I shall miss you.'

'I'll never be far away. If ever you need me, I will come to you.' With a sigh, the old woman stroked the still wet curls before continuing with her task.

Once Seraphina's hair was dry, the dressing of the bride began. She was laced into her corset, and petticoats of the finest lawn were tied round her waist, followed by an underskirt of white silk embroidered with silver thread. Over this came a white silk dress cut so low that her breasts brimmed over the top of her bodice, their swelling fullness scarcely hidden under a fichu of the most delicate lace. More lace fell from her sleeves, so soft and light that it felt like the merest touch of thistledown.

Silver ribbons were threaded through her hair. If it had been summer there would have been white roses too, but this was the depths of winter and there were no flowers to be had.

'Now the necklace,' Megan said, going to the chest for Brandon's gift.

Seraphina wrinkled her nose. 'No. Not that. I want my mother's pearls.'

Megan stopped, the lid half open. 'His Lordship sent the necklace for your wedding day.'

'So what? I will not wear his jewel. The Ladies of Witchcraven always wear pearls on their wedding day, just as they always wear white to signify their connection with the moon and the gift of their maiden self.'

Seraphina reached up and pulled the ribbons from her hair. 'I will have pearls in my hair and around my neck.'

'So you shall, and rightly said,' Megan cried. 'No man will tell you what to do.' She twisted the pearls into Seraphina's hair, then fastened another rope around her neck.

'Show me,' Seraphina demanded. So far she had refused to look at herself, but now she was ready.

Triumphantly Megan held up the mirror, framing a portrait of a lady in white silk, who stared out of the glass like some faery creature, distant and remote. Her green eyes were fringed with long dark lashes. A faint blush spread across her cheekbones. She held her head high. The rope of pearls around her slender neck. Her almost naked breasts only partly concealed by a drift of gossamer lace. The bodice of her dress coming into a narrow waist, which billowed out into a full skirt. She was mysterious, untouched. Exactly as she wanted to be.

'Oh, my little one.' Megan wiped tears from her eyes.

'Damn me! A veritable angel, by God,' Sir Greville exclaimed as his daughter appeared at the head of the stairs. Bewigged and powdered, dressed in rich blue silk, he swayed slightly as he stared up at her, his slack red mouth half open.

'Then you approve,' Seraphina said coolly, and began to descend.

Her father nodded. Sweat stood on his forehead and, pulling his sleeve across his face, he fumbled for the flask he had hidden in the skirts of his coat.

'You are your mother come again,' he said. 'And as cold and as strange,' he muttered as she reached his side.

Seraphina inclined her head, pretending she had not

heard those last words; but she had, and instead of upsetting her, it made her glad that she appeared remote, untouched by lust or desire. Just the image she wanted to present to her new husband.

Let him regret the moment he set eyes on me. Until I choose different, she resolved, as she took her father's arm and let him lead her to the waiting carriage.

8

The trees were laced with ice as they drove to the village church. There were deep shadows in the lanes, but high above the ancient circle of stones the sun shone, a white disc, silver as the moon in the blue sky.

A good omen, Seraphina thought as she sat still and silent at her father's side. *It shows that the Goddess smiles on this enterprise and will help me in what I plan for tonight.*

Along their route people came to their doors to see the bride. Men doffed their hats, women curtseyed and children waved, or ran after the horses, laughing and shouting. Some houses were decked with holly and ivy in a sign that those within worshipped the Goddess; in others people made do with fluttering of handkerchiefs or waving of scarves as the finely-turned-out horses and carriage passed.

Outside the lych gate the driver pulled up. The steps were lowered and, after another quick swig from his hip flask, Sir Greville heaved himself from his seat and descended. Once firmly on the ground, he turned to help his daughter alight. Relieved to be out of the close confines of the carriage and away from the fumes of her father's brandy, Seraphina took a deep breath. The sharp air slid down her throat like bubbly wine, invigorating her and giving her the courage to face what must come next. In spite of this she did not hurry as her father led her to the church door, and once in the porch she paused to absorb the alien atmosphere.

St Margaret's was a place she rarely entered. Sir Greville, as was his duty as lord of the manor, regularly attended the services; his daughter did not. The parish excused her on the grounds that she was a motherless orphan and that the Ladies of Witchcraven had always been peculiar in that respect. In the meantime she slept late on Sundays, but was careful to make sure there was a good dinner ready for her father on his return, so that his anger at the length of the parson's sermon would not rebound on her.

'Come along, my dear.' Sir Greville appeared as eager to get through the ceremony as she was.

The trumpeter in the church orchestra blew a fanfare, the fiddles started up, and her father led her into the church. In contrast to the brightness outside, the building was dark and damp. Forced to take part in this marriage ritual, Seraphina felt a shiver of fear slide up her spine. The ancient holiness of the building oppressed her. She sensed centuries of Christian prayer and worship that had seeped into the very stones and threatened to engulf her. A faint whiff of incense choked her, the scent of candle wax and closely-gathered humanity rose to her nostrils, causing her to sway as if she might faint.

'Steady now, steady,' Sir Greville murmured, as if soothing a frightened horse.

Heads turned, voices whispered. Lifting her head high, Seraphina sailed haughtily down the aisle. The pews were full, but the people appeared to her no more solid than shadows. There was a rustling and murmuring, heads turned and she caught the odd comment.

'A fine filly, that niece of mine,' her uncle Sir Aubrey Fitzgerald said.

'A strange choice of dress, but her mother was the same. Headstrong, self-willed,' her aunt Harriet added.

'She looks ...' Harry's voice faltered, and she almost sensed his pain, then shut it out from her mind as she reached the altar, which some of the village women had decorated with boughs of evergreen. These were so abundant that they almost hid the simple brass cross, but nothing could conceal the stained glass that rose above the altar.

I will not be ill, Seraphina vowed to herself as she joined her bridegroom. *I will do what I must and say what I must, and soon I shall be back out in the sunlight.*

She kept her eyes firmly in front of her, refusing even to glance at the dark shape of Lord Brandon beside her. She was aware only that he was dressed in his customary black silk. Darkness and light, merging together. There was something so right about this elemental union. But she would not think of it. Her light would conquer his dark. Lifting her head even higher, she fixed her glance on a square of deep blue stained glass.

The parson shuffled forward. Her father relinquished her arm, her hand was placed in Lord Brandon's. She felt the warmth of his skin, but there was no other response; he let her fingers lie loosely in his. Seraphina's lips tightened. So this was the game he was playing; pretending that he was not in the slightest stirred by the presence of his young and nubile bride. Swallowing her anger, she sighed softly, then moved her shoulders so that the lace at her breast fluttered. Lord Bandon's grip tightened momentarily. Seraphina gave a tiny cry. Her eyelids fluttered and she swayed a little toward him, instantly straightening up when his head turned toward her. So, he was not as impervious to her as he wanted to appear. A smile played around her lips, only to be swiftly suppressed as the parson began to speak.

'Do you, Seraphina de Lacy, take this man, George Fitzwilliam Brandon, to be your lawful wedded husband? Do you vow to love, honour and obey ...'

The words droned on, until finally the parson had finished and was waiting for her response. Seraphina took a tiny breath. Part of her wanted to pick up her skirts and run as fast and as far from this place as she could. Another, harder, self told her to draw out the moment, to make both the groom and the congregation wait for her to agree to the bargain she was making. She felt the man beside her stiffen with anger. His mouth narrowed, his nostrils flared. She was sure that if they had not been in a place he thought of as scared he would have struck her, or seized her by the shoulders and shaken her until she choked out the words she was refusing to say.

That would show them. Her father, the people in the church, her aunt, her uncle, her darling Harry. Laughter bubbled to her lips and she pressed them together. She waited for one more beat of the heart, then said in a clear, cool voice, as if there had been no question of any hesitation, 'I do.'

There was a muttering, a rustling, a relaxing of tension in the church. Then Lord Brandon was saying his vows. The orchestra piped up again and the bridal couple walked arm in arm down the aisle to the sound of clapping and congratulations. Once outside, there was barely time for her to take a reviving breath of winter air before she was being lifted into the Brandon carriage for the short drive back to Witchcraven Manor.

'Thank the Lord that's over,' her husband said shortly.

'My lord!' Seraphina looked up at him wide-eyed. She had decided to play the part of the innocent bride to the hilt. 'Whatever do you mean?'

'You can stop your playacting. It does not convince.'

'But I …' Seraphina began, then stopped. Taming this man was going to prove more difficult than she had thought, and more exciting. More challenging too, and she had always relished a challenge. She lowered her head to hide her smile, but Lord Brandon had already turned his face from her, and he stared fixedly out of the window until they arrived at Witchcraven.

The footman held open the door, and immediately Lord Brandon's whole attitude toward Seraphina changed. Jumping from the carriage, he offered her his hand. Seraphina hesitated. Framed by the door of the carriage was her beloved house. Its thick stone walls, its deep-set windows with their strangely curved panes that distorted everything you saw. The doors were of thick oak, barred with iron; the slate roof hung low over the whole building, protecting it and all who lived in it from the wild weather that swept down from the moors, at the same time hiding its secrets from those who must not know. It was the house that had kept her safe, allowed her to grow into the person she was, to take up her place in the world. The next day, she must leave her beloved manor, if not forever then for weeks, months, maybe even years, because she had married this man and must go and live with him.

'My lady,' Brandon prompted.

Seraphina blinked away a sudden unexpected tear and, losing patience with her, Brandon clasped his hands around her waist and swung her to the ground. His grip was hard and firm, his face set. Drawn by his aura of mastery, Seraphina half closed her eyes. This was a man who knew what he wanted and would let no-one stand in his way. She had only to soften, only to let herself slip into his arms and … And she would be lost.

'Thank you, my lord, but I can stand on my own two feet,' she said, walking away from him toward the main door of the house, which stood, as tradition demanded, wide open to welcome them.

'I'm sure you can,' she heard him say, but did not look back. Instead she stepped inside and turned to greet him as he came into the stone-flagged entrance hall. She wanted to make sure he knew that she was the mistress here.

The main hall of the house had been set for the wedding feast. In this, the oldest part of the building, the ceiling soared up to the very roof. The beams that supported it were carved with ancient symbols, and the moon and stars had once been painted between them. Over the centuries they had faded, as had the wall painting, which showed a beautiful woman dressed in white, a halo of moonlight around her head, a white hare at her feet and behind her the outline of the stone circle that looked down on the manor from the uplands. As the years had gone by, the sacred image had become covered by a patina of smoke and dirt, and only those who knew where to look could trace the figure of the Goddess and bow their heads in a swift and secret recognition of her power in this house.

Swags of evergreens had been hung on the walls. A fire blazed in the hearth, filling the air with the scent of pine. Candles had been lit to hold at bay the rapidly dying winter light, and their light flickered over the polished surfaces of the tables, which had been set with the best silver and plate that Sir Greville could muster. Much of this was borrowed from Sir Aubrey and Lady Harriet, as were the rich damask tablecloths and silver candelabra that stood on the high table, where the bride and groom and the most important guests would sit.

There was plenty of room for the other guests on the tables that filled the main body of the hall. Harry was at one of these. The expression on his face was so grim that Seraphina feared he had not got her message. As she passed him, his eyes met hers. It was only the briefest of glances, but as she raised an enquiring eyebrow, his face broke into a grin and he winked. Getting to his feet, he held out his hand to Lord Brandon.

'Let me congratulate you on this happy occasion,' he cried. His lordship bowed his head swiftly in acknowledgement, and would have moved on to join his wife, who was waiting for him, but Harry was not ready to let him go. 'You have stolen the most beautiful woman in the whole county from the rest of us miserable, unworthy creatures,' he continued. Seraphina had to bite her lip to stop herself from giggling. 'However, my cousin Seraphina is so dear to me that I must wish you both all the joy that you deserve.'

There was a brief growl from his lordship. Harry sat down again, and Seraphina almost burst in her attempt not to laugh.

Bride and groom sat side by side at the high table.

Before the feasting could begin, Megan approached carrying a platter on which stood a small dish of salt and one of bread. She offered it first to the groom and then to the bride. Lord Brandon took his piece of bread and dipped it in the salt; then, without being told, he held it out to Seraphina. She took a bite, then did the same for him.

'May you forever have all that you need and all that you want. Both of this world and the other,' Megan murmured softly.

Lord Brandon bowed his head; a brief, almost unnoticeable bow that only Seraphina appeared to see. She glanced quickly at Megan. Had the old woman coached him in what to do and say? And if so, why? Didn't she know what Seraphina had in mind for her husband that night? And was it not obvious that she had no intention of treating him as the rightful consort of the Lady of Witchcraven? Frowning, she tried to catch her nurse's eye.

'I think you could at least summon up a smile,' Lord Brandon said coldly.

'Why should that be, my lord? Do you think that perhaps I am not truly happy in this marriage?' Seraphina's voice was full of sarcasm.

'Whether or not you are, I expect you to behave in public as if you were a happy bride,' his lordship replied.

'Which, of course, I am. My joy knows no bounds.' Seraphina batted her eyelashes and smiled up at her husband.

Lord Brandon's hands tightened round the stem of his glass, the knuckles white with fury. For a moment Seraphina thought he would break it, but then he forced himself to loosen his grip.

'Mine also,' he said in a low tone. 'I will show you how much when this farce is over and we are alone in our chamber.'

'Farce!' Seraphina cried. 'When I and my servants have worked so hard to prepare this wedding breakfast, at such a dull time of year and in so short a time?'

'I am sure you have done very well.' His lordship turned from her, apparently bored with the way their conversation was going. He rose to his feet and held up his glass. 'My friends! May I welcome you all to this wedding feast.'

There was a roar of approval, and glasses were raised and toasts proposed. Men and women too drank deeply. Harry, Seraphina noted a little anxiously, was quickly flushed with drink. Lord Brandon however appeared totally untouched, and she herself made sure to take only one or two sips. For the rest she raised her glass to her lips and pretended to drink.

Nor did she eat much. The feast lasted long into the evening. Dish followed dish, until candles began to gutter and the night shadows drew in. Her guests dined on finest venison, partridge, beef and mutton, a cold collation and hot pies and puddings, followed by trifles and junkets and sweetmeats of all sorts. Only Seraphina limited herself to just a few bites of game and a candied plum or two.

Every course was washed down with much wine, and as the time drew on, the company became increasingly merry. Coats and wigs were discarded, men sprawled over tables, women leaned amorously against their partners or someone else's. The women's curls hung limp, sweat trickled down between their breasts, and they used their fans, waving them slowly, sensuously, spelling out messages of desire and assignation.

Sir Greville, scarlet faced, belched and roared at the coarse jokes of his cronies. Even Sir Aubrey unbent a little and managed a snigger or two, while Lady Harriet leaned back in her chair, legs spread wide, and demanded her glass be filled and refilled so that she could drink to the health of the bride and groom. And the lucky escape of her son.

Seraphina, catching the last comment, which was intended as a whisper, lifted her hand to her mouth and smiled. She nodded graciously at her aunt, who stared back at her in puzzlement. Then Seraphina turned back to her husband and did her best to gaze up at him in adoration. It was easier than she had expected. Unlike the other men in the room, Lord Brandon was still in control of himself and his emotions. His glance, when he looked at the dissipation that surrounded them, was one of both disgust and contempt for the sweating, heaving bodies; and yet beneath that arrogant exterior Seraphina sensed a deeper, more passionate sensuality. He, like her, did not want to play at lovemaking; he wanted to explore, to dive deep into as yet unplumbed depths. To conquer and be conquered.

His eye caught hers. Was there the faintest hint of a smile on those lips? Did he know what she was thinking? To her fury, Seraphina felt her colour rise. 'The heat,' she said, fanning herself with her hand.

Scanning the tables in front of her, she found Harry. *Look at me*, she willed him. *Put down that glass and look.*

Her cousin shook his head as if wrestling with some difficult idea. He yawned loudly and stretched his arms above his head, like a man in desperate need of sleep. Then, just as she was beginning to despair, he pushed back his chair and, swaying to his feet, announced to one and all that he was going for a piss. Before he stumbled out of the room, however, he stared straight at the bride and swept her a half-mocking bow.

'To the bride, the bloody beautiful bride,' he slurred.

'Your cousin Harry appears the worse for wear,' Lord Brandon remarked coolly.

'So do most of the men in the room,' Seraphina said coldly.

'The women too. Except for you.'

'I have no need of wine or spirits.'

'No, you do not. Your blood is hot enough.'

'It is the heat of the fire, the press of so many bodies.'

'Are you then in need of a breath of cooler air?' Lord Brandon said; but his eyes sent another message, and Seraphina had to look away at the thought of being stripped naked by that dark gaze.

She reached blindly for her glass, and her hand inadvertently brushed against his. The touch of his skin against hers sent a wave of such intensity vibrating through her body that she gave a gasp of shock – or was it desire?

Even as the sound left her lips, he raised a quizzical eyebrow. Leaning toward her, one arm around her shoulder, his fingers resting on her rapidly heaving breast, he whispered, 'Is it time for bed, my lady? This has been a long day, and tonight promises to be longer still.'

'The night is still young. Our guests are enjoying themselves,' Seraphina said, staring straight ahead of her.

'Then it is time for us to do the same.' His lips nuzzled at her neck.

Her breathing quickened. A deep, warm flood of desire swept over her. She wanted nothing more than to hold up her arms to him, to let him sweep her off her feet and carry her from the hall.

'If that is what your lordship wishes.'

With a short, sharp gesture she brushed him away. She stood up, her white dress gleaming in the candlelight, and smiled at the drunken mass of people in front of her.

'I bid you goodnight,' she cried, her voice clear and cool in the hot, greasy air.

'I too.' Lord Brandon was at her side. His grip was firm on her arm as he led her through the ranks of leering, ribald guests and out into the entrance hall.

'Your chamber, my lady.' There was an urgency in his voice that sent her blood racing. 'Where the bloody hell is it? Truly this custom of spending the wedding night in the bride's house is a damned inconvenient one.'

'Maybe.' Seraphina had recovered herself a little. 'But that is how it has always been done at Witchcraven. Just be grateful that there are no jesting groomsmen or knowing women to light us to bed. Come.'

She did not hold out her hand to him as she would have done to any other man but, taking the candle that had been left for her, with a swish of her silken skirts she led him up the stone staircase.

At the top, the house branched into the two wings of the building that embraced the central courtyard. On the left-hand side were the rooms used by the family, including Seraphina's bedroom and Sir Greville's, while on the right were the formal apartments. The latter were never occupied, rarely swept or dusted, but that night it was to the right that Seraphina turned. Her candle threw long shadows onto the panelled walls behind them: hers slim and graceful; his taller, broader, striding behind her like some dark being.

At the door of the great chamber she stopped, but only long enough to lift the latch. With a different husband she would have waited for him to carry her over the threshold, but not with Lord Brandon. With him she must remain dominant. Anything that hinted that he rather than she was in control she could not allow.

Stepping inside, she checked quickly to see that everything was in place. In preparation for the wedding night, Megan had had the dingy room transformed. Candles burned on the mantelpiece, and the fire crackled with logs and sweet-smelling herbs that filled the room with the scent of lavender, rosemary and summer. The tapestries that hung in the alcoves in place of cupboards had been beaten clean of dust and dirt. The floorboards gleamed with polish, and silk curtains embroidered with moons and stars hung at the windows and around the four-poster bed. There was a jug and a basin of hot water on a table at the foot of the bed, and on the old carved chest by the window stood a flagon and two goblets of rare Venetian glass.

'At last we are alone.' Lord Brandon's voice was husky with desire.

'Indeed we are.' Seraphina looked up at him, then quickly lowered her eyes as an innocent maiden would surely do.

'Come here.' He moved toward her and would have taken her in his arms; but she was ready for him and stepped quickly to one side.

'A toast first, my lord.'

'A toast! For God's sake have we not had enough of toasting to last us the night? Now is not the time to drink. Now –' He stopped suddenly as Seraphina glided close and put a finger on his lips.

'Now is the time for love,' she murmured. 'But first I want us to drink to our future happiness. My father,' she moved away before he could stop her, 'set aside this bottle of wine on the day I was born. He said it came from grapes grown on the island of Venus's birth.'

Taking the flagon, she pulled the stopper from its slender neck and poured the wine into the two glasses. Holding one out to him, she said, 'Drink with me, my lord, and the goddess of love will surely bless our union.'

'Now there's a toast I will make!' Brandon seized the glass from her hand.

She waited, hoping that he would down the drink immediately, but instead he watched as she took the other glass and held it up. The scarlet glass glowed in the firelight. The heady scent of the wine rose to their nostrils.

'To us,' Seraphina said. 'To you and to me.' She lifted the glass to her lips.

'To us,' her husband echoed, and drank.

She bent her head, pretending to take a sip. She licked her tongue over her moist lips and, tipping back her head, exposed her slender white neck.

'My lord,' she murmured, and swayed a little as if the wine she had pretended to drink had gone to her head. As she had intended, he caught her round the waist and pulled her toward him.

'No fainting now, my lady. That must wait –' his lips were on her neck, his teeth grazing her skin '– until you faint with pleasure.'

Seraphina sighed. She felt him harden against her

and pressed her body closer to his. She fluttered her eyelashes and, winding her arms around his neck, sighed again. Then she peeled herself away.

'My dress,' she whispered. 'Unlace me. Quick.'

His breath was coming fast, but his fingers were swift and experienced. Her outer dress slipped from her shoulders. One pull of her ribbon and her underskirt slid to the floor. Kicking them free, she stepped out in nothing but her petticoat and corset.

Brandon flung off his coat, his shirt. She knelt and unbuttoned his britches, freeing him, then kneeling back as if overawed by the sight of his cock, huge and firm. It was indeed magnificent, and she longed to twine her fingers round it, stroke it, smooth it, then slide her lips over it; but he had her by the elbows and was lifting her onto her feet, forcing her back toward the bed. Seraphina cast a glance at the flagon on the chest. Surely she had poured him enough? Half a glass, Megan had said, and to be on the safe side she had given him more.

'On your back, my lady,' he commanded, and she felt herself falling.

'Oh,' she cried, as if in fright, and rolled quickly to one side.

She held out her arms, and he was beside her, naked, strong, eager. His mouth was on hers, his kisses hard, demanding, his tongue searching, forcing its way through her lips. She couldn't help herself: she was wet and hot. Her legs were parting. She wanted him. She wanted his cock inside her, pushing and thrusting its way into her deepest, most secret places.

'Seraphina,' he sighed. His eyes shut, his breathing slowed. As suddenly as if he had been knocked unconscious, he rolled over onto his back and slept.

Seraphina waited until she was absolutely sure that he was beyond waking, then she sat up. Cupping her breasts in her hands, she let her fingers close over her nipples. They stood hard and firm on the smooth globes of her breasts. A quick pinch brought a quiver of pleasure between her legs. She bit her lip, and a delighted giggle rose to her mouth. Totally and utterly naked, the firelight playing on her white skin, on the dark triangle between her legs, the thick tresses of her hair that fell down her back, she walked over to the alcove at the side of the bed and pulled the curtain aside.

'Harry,' she said, and flung her arms around his neck. He was already naked, his golden fairness in vivid contrast to the darkness of her sleeping husband.

'Seraph,' he groaned. 'Thank the Lord. Another moment and I would not have been able to hold back.'

'Me neither. All day I have been waiting for this. You saw me looking at you. Looking and lusting. I am hot for you,' she panted. 'Take me. Take me now.'

She kissed him, her mouth wide, her tongue thrusting between his lips. He hoisted her up, she wound her legs around his waist. His sex throbbed against her belly; then, as she slid herself down onto him, it was inside her. Even as he entered her she felt her muscles close around him, contracting, slowly at first, then faster and faster, with an eager, greedy, triumphant pleasure that brought her quickly to her conclusion; and as she came, so did he, with an almighty great shout.

She did not stop him. She did nothing to quieten him. She did not care. If Brandon woke from his drug-induced sleep and saw them, so be it. To be cuckolded on his wedding night was what he deserved. He was simply paying for having treated her like an object, a possession without needs or feelings.

But the potion Megan had made was strong and powerful, and beyond a faint flutter of his eyelids, his lordship did not stir. He was sleeping soundly as a baby when Seraphina, sliding free of her lover, ran to the bed and jumped on the mattress, crouching there like some wild creature. Her hair cascading round her body, hiding the curves of her firm white flesh, she glanced up at Harry and beckoned him to come to her.

With one wild bound he was beside her, wrestling her onto her back. 'Got you,' he cried.

'Shhh,' she whispered. 'You must not wake my lord and master.'

'I don't give a damn for your so-called lord. I'll show you who is master in this bed.'

Harry's lips descended on hers. His body arched over her, his cock hard, already preparing to thrust between her legs.

'Not so soon!' Seraphina's hand curled round the erect member. Her fingers slid up and down over the smooth surface of his sheath. 'Did I say I was ready?' she whispered in his ear. 'Did I say you could have me? Wait there, you rogue, you stealer of other men's wives.'

Wriggling her shoulders free, she pushed him gently so that he rolled off her and lay on his side, facing her. Kissing him gently on his lips, running her hands through his hair, she curled one leg around his hips, positioning herself so that the tip of his cock grazed against the lips of her vagina.

The mingled scent of their juices rose between them. Her skin glowed like rose petals in the firelight; her dark hair tumbled over her shoulders and onto her breasts. She kissed him again, more passionately now. Her tongue darted in between his lips. He tasted of wine and feasting and Harry.

'Oh, my dearest cousin,' she sighed; and positioning her hips so that he could slide easily into her, she let him enter. Eyes half closed, she watched the man sleeping beside them, let her glance linger on the chiselled features, the broad shoulders, the narrow waist. He was so handsome, so virile. If she reached over she could take his cock in her hand, squeeze and stroke and rub until he …

'Oh!' she gasped as her orgasm took her. 'Oh!' she cried again as Harry spent himself inside her and she was shaken by another wave of intense pleasure. 'Oh,' she murmured, as sleepy and satisfied as a cat. Reaching out, she tangled her fingers in Brandon's hair, pulling at the thick dark locks, almost willing him to wake. To find them, to take her.

'We showed him. Just as you said we would.' Harry yawned and grinned.

'We did.' Seraphina kissed him lightly.

'I have to go.' Harry began to get up.

'Not yet. The night is young.' Seraphina stretched her arms above her head so that her nipples rose enticingly. 'Or rather, the dawn has not yet come. Who knows what we might still have time for?'

'We might indeed, but right now I am mighty sleepy.'

'Then sleep for an hour or two.' Seraphina took his hand and pulled him down so that he lay on the other side of her. Lying between the two men, she wriggled deeper into the mattress and, smiling, closed her eyes.

She did not intend to sleep for long, but the exertions of the night had tired her and she slipped swiftly into her dreams.

A thin shaft of morning sun, piercing its way through the silken curtains of the bed, eventually woke her. She lay on her back, one hand across Brandon's chest, the other curled lightly around Harry's flaccid cock.

'My lady.' Megan stood at the bottom of the bed. 'He must go.'

'No.' Seraphina shook her head, relishing the feel of her hair against her bare skin. 'Rather let him come. Again and again. Let them both,' she giggled.

Her grip on Harry's cock tightened, her fingers began to move. He stirred, his eyes opened, he turned toward her.

'Seraph,' he began, and stopped. Brandon's breathing had changed.

'Hurry, hurry!' Megan said urgently. 'He's waking. The potion will hold him no longer. Come on, master Harry, get into your clothes and run; or gather your clothes and run. There's no more time.'

She pulled the sheet that half covered him from their naked bodies and shook her head impatiently as Harry grabbed his clothes from the alcove where he had discarded them the previous night and started to pull his trousers on.

'No, no. There is no time,' the old woman scolded. 'Take your boots and go.'

'Don't fuss, Megan. He will not be caught. I'll see to that.'

Turning on her side, Seraphina lifted herself on one elbow and, lowering her head, kissed the waking Brandon on the lips. Her hair fell over both their faces, cloaking them so that Harry's rush to the door, clutching his boots, shirt and coat, could not be seen.

Lord Brandon's dark eyes opened drowsily, then a momentary frown creased his forehead. 'Seraphina?' he said, puzzled.

'My lord. Who else should it be? Surely you do not expect to wake with some other woman at your side on our wedding day?'

The door of the chamber shut softly and she sat up and, looking down at him, pulled a face.

'I don't know.' Brandon struggled to sit up, then fell back on his pillow. 'Ye gods, my head. What the devil was in that wine we drank last night?'

'Nothing but grapes from the island of the goddess of love,' Seraphina assured him.

'Potent stuff, then. I trust it was good for you.'

'Oh yes,' she smiled. 'It was.' From the side of the room she heard Megan suppress a chuckle. 'I should wash and dress. Megan has brought hot water.' She began to slide toward the edge of the bed. Her feet had just touched the bare boards when his arm snaked out and gripped her wrist.

'I gave you pleasure, did I?' His fingers closed round her flesh. Nails bit into her skin. 'And did you do the same for me, my lady?'

'I should hope I did.' The words were modest, but Seraphina was using all her strength to try to shake him off. He, however, was too strong for her.

'Get out,' he growled at Megan. 'Your mistress and I have some unfinished business to attend to.'

'Megan, no.' Seraphina struggled to free herself, but Lord Brandon held her down on the bed, both wrists pinioned now as she lay on her back, his furious face above her. 'Don't go,' she begged the old woman. She tried to lift her head, but his lips were on hers, hard and cruel, the kisses so violent that they left her breathless.

'Lie there,' he commanded, as the door shut after Megan. He leapt from the bed and she followed, but before she could reach him, he was already at the door, turning the key in the lock, and she knew she did not have the strength to take it from him.

'How dare you!' she blazed, standing naked before him. 'Unlock the door at once. You cannot make me a prisoner in my own house.'

'You are my wife. I can do what I wish. When and where I choose,' he snarled. He strode over toward her, his penis fully erect. She backed away. He loomed over her. His cock grazed her belly, and she felt her legs weaken. The size of him, the strength of him, inflamed her. Yet she would not give in. What she wanted was to have him on his back, hands bound to the bedposts, she straddling him, hips thrusting, cunt contracting, in and out, riding him like the stallion he had given her until her pleasure was done.

'Get on the bed,' he ordered.

'I will not!'

Forcing herself to stay upright, she met and held his gaze.

'You will!'

In one swift movement he took her arm, twisted her round, then pushed her so that she fell face down on the mattress.

'On your knees,' he commanded.

Seraphina did not move. His hand came between her legs. She moved against the hardness of his fingers, but there was to be no release, for he hoisted her up so that she was on all fours like a farmyard animal, and without another word he thrust himself inside her.

'There,' he said. 'And there. I shall have my way with you, my lady, whether you will or no. I will take you in any way I please, and may you deny me at your peril.'

'Never,' she gasped, but whether it was in denial or agreement she no longer knew.

With each hard jerk inside her, she contracted around him. Even as her mind and soul fought him, her body welcomed his. She was coming, her orgasm was gathering force, she was melting beneath him, she was …

With one final deliberate thrust he shot into her. Withdrawing, he bent over her and fastened his teeth on her neck. Seraphina whimpered as he bit into the flesh. Her first frustrated wave intensified, but even as he sensed her arousal, he flung her face down on the bed.

She lay there, wounded and needy, Brandon looming above her with a strange expression on his face: a mixture of triumph, satisfaction and yet sorrow, as if in spite of the pleasure he had obviously experienced, there was something lacking in what he had done.

Was it that he had wanted her to come? Catching a fleeting glimpse of his face as she struggled onto her back, Seraphina doubted it. His lordship was an accomplished and experienced lover who would make sure that his partner came to her climax if he wished it. So he had not wished it. Was this part of his game? Of the unacknowledged war they were waging? Leaving her frustrated, did he now expect her to beg? Well, he would not have that satisfaction. Hiding as much of herself as she could with her hair, Seraphina crossed her arms across her breasts.

'I think I will dress now,' she said, a little shakily.

'I think not. You have not come to your conclusion. I would not want you to spend your day in an agony of frustration.'

Thinking furiously, Seraphina bowed her head. What did he expect her to do? She did not want him to see her bewilderment.

'Pleasure yourself, my lady.' Brandon's voice was soft and sensual. 'Bring yourself off, as I know you are wont to do.' His tongue flicked over his lips. His eyes narrowed, his nostrils widened.

'I will not.' Seraphina shrank back against the pillows, pressing her thighs together.

'Then you will stay here until you do. Remember I have the key to this room. I am master here and can do as I like. No servant will dare defy me for fearing of losing their place. Not even your faithful old Megan. So go on, do what you long to do. Give yourself the release you crave.' His voice softened again. 'I will watch you as your hand falls from your breast, as it moves slowly down the roundness of your belly. See, feel, the softness of your skin beneath your touch. There, there already your limbs are loosening. Now tighten your fingers round that rosebud of a nipple. Gently at first, like a baby nuzzling at the breast, then firmer, pinch and pull. Do you feel the tug between your legs, the pleasure gathering inside you?'

'Oh yes,' Seraphina gasped. 'I do.'

'Hush,' he murmured. 'Do not speak. Listen. Lean back against the pillows. Good. Spread your legs, slide your hand to the top of your mound. There. Tangle your fingers in the dampness of your hair, let the curls wind around your fingers, pull a little. No, do not let them find their way inside you, however eager they are. Not until I say. Not until I …'

'My lord …' Seraphina's thumb was on her clitoris. Circling, pressing. But he had her by the wrist.

Stopping the pressure, denying the entrance. 'No!' she cried.

'Yes.' His fingers were inside her. Thumb on her clitoris, forefingers exploring. 'You are ready.' Withdrawing his hand. 'Now, my lady, now.'

Pressing herself back against the bed, too far gone even to need a touch, she came.

'Good,' he said, in the tone a teacher might use to a well-behaved pupil. 'You have done what you were told.'

'I ...' Seraphina began, instinctively opening her legs as he came closer. To her surprise and fury, he did nothing, merely stood there looking down on her. Her body was flushed and warm, she smelled of him and of herself. She knew that she looked enticing, that he was far from unwilling, but he made no move toward her. Instead he looked her over, his gaze raking her nakedness from the tips of her toes, up over her calves, the tautness of her thighs, the curls of dark hair, wet with their come, then up over her belly, her breasts, her shoulders. Finally his eyes met hers.

For a long moment he held her glance, and once again she found herself unable to read those unfathomable eyes. She thought she saw the same suppressed fury that was evident in the cruel curve of his mouth, the arrogance that showed itself in the uplifted eyebrow, as if she was some sort of lower being he had been asked to view and give an opinion on. Beneath all that, however, she suspected some other emotion, and for one wild moment she thought it was a deep, untouchable sorrow. Then he looked away. The moment was gone and she was left lying naked on their marriage bed, while her husband of barely a few hours turned away and was coolly and calmly dressing himself.

'You are leaving me already?' The words sprang to her lips.

'I have business to attend to.' His attention was focused on tucking his shirt into his britches. 'I will be at Brandon Hall, if you should want me.'

'Brandon Hall? But it's our honeymoon. I'm your bride. I should be there with you.'

'Indeed you are my wife.' His tone made this sound as if it was a surprising idea. 'Lady Brandon should be with her husband. You, however, madam –'

'I what?' Seraphina interrupted, leaping out of bed. Hair tumbling to her waist, she confronted him furiously.

'I do not think that you yet see yourself as fully my wife,' he said.

Seraphina stared at him dumbfounded. 'After what passed between us, last night and this morning?' she finally managed to stammer.

'Ah yes, last night.' His lordship looked at her, his eyes hooded. 'Do you know,' he said in a conversational tone, that sounded casual and friendly enough but that sent the ice flowing through her blood, 'I had a very strange dream last night.'

'A dream, my lord? No doubt the result of too much rich food and wine,' Seraphina suggested hopefully.

'Wine? How could that be? I drank very little. Except of course the loving cup prepared by your faithful old nurse.'

'Megan?' *The potion wasn't strong enough. Goddess help me.*

'The very same. If I dreamed and the wine was to blame, then it was a strong potion indeed.'

Seraphina's stomach clenched, and for a moment she

thought she was going to be sick.

'On the other hand, perhaps it proved a blessing. Perhaps the dreams it prompted showed me something about my new wife.'

'What could that have been?' Seraphina raised her head and looked at him haughtily. Whatever he thought of her, whatever he might have seen or guessed, this man was not going to get the better of her.

'I dreamed that as we lay together, another came between us. He took his pleasure of you and you took yours of him.'

'My lord, how could that have happened? No-one would have dared come into our chamber.'

Even to her own ears, Seraphina's protests sounded feeble and unconvincing. As if despising her words, Brandon turned his head and looked out of the window at the new day.

'I have a feeling, my lady, that whatever you want, you will attempt to make happen,' he said in a voice low with menace. Turning back to her, he said, 'That, however, will not work with me. I bid you good day.' And turning on his heel, he left her.

9

'Megan!' Seraphina screamed. 'Megan, he knows!' she cried as the old woman came hurrying into the room. 'Lord Brandon knows what I, what Harry and I, did last night, in that very bed. Oh, how can that be?' She sank down on the stool by the fire and put her head in her hands.

'Now stop your fretting.' Megan pulled a blanket from the bed and wrapped it round Seraphina's shoulders.

'I'm not fretting, I'm worried and furious.' Seraphina threw back the cover; then, remembering Brandon's cold look and unreadable eyes, she shivered and drew it around herself again.

'That's better. There's no need to risk a chill,' Megan said.

'A chill! I'm more likely to be burning up from a fever. A fever of fury.' Seraphina thumped her fist on her thigh. 'I meant to humiliate him – not in his eyes, for he was fast asleep, or so I thought, but in my own. And what happened? He saw it all, and now he has humiliated me!'

Her colour rose, and she flushed from her toes to the

top of her head as she remembered how coldly he had treated her, how he had watched with such detachment as she had come in that final climax. The one he had induced by his soft words. 'He had me where he wanted me,' she groaned.

'And it was not flat on your back with his thing between your legs?' Megan chuckled.

'No!' Seraphina leapt to her feet. 'That, although it was not what I had planned, would have been a better outcome. He will not get away with this. I will show him that I cannot be treated like some serving wench who will do anything to service her master's pleasure.'

'I'm sure you will. My lady always gets what she wants in the end,' Megan said soothingly as Seraphina paced angrily around the chamber. 'But that is not the way,' she added as Seraphina banged her fists against the bedposts. 'You stop that this minute!' She ran forward and grabbed Seraphina by the wrists as she was about to butt the carved wood with her head. 'A great big bruise will do your looks no good. Now sit down, let me bring you a calming drink of valerian and some hot water to wash the temper and –' she sniffed the air '– the scent of come from your body. Then I will bring fresh linen and you will dress and have your hair done so that you will look the very lady when you go to him.'

'Go to him!' Seraphina snarled. 'That is the last thing I will do. He will come to me, or I shall never see him again.'

'Tut, tut,' Megan clicked her tongue. 'Such fine and haughty words. Which, as I've told you before, will butter you no parsnips, if Lord Brandon, as you suspect, has indeed seen what he should not. Though how that could have happened I do not know, for the potion I brewed was good and strong. It would have felled a lesser man and sent him to sleep for a week; but I had a good look at his lordship's body, and those shoulders, those buttocks, those legs, they all told me he had the strength and stamina to need a deeper spell, a more powerful infusion.'

'Yes, yes,' Seraphina interrupted. 'We know all this. And,' she lifted her head proudly, 'I am resolved. I will not beg or plead. If he comes to me, he comes to beg my forgiveness or not at all.'

'For the Goddess's sake, where will that get you?' Megan threw up her hands in exasperation. 'If you want to have this man where you want him – and I wager you'll enjoy the game of getting him there – then you must go about it in a much more clever way. Do what he does not expect. Play the game your way. Wrong-foot him at every turn, just as you planned.'

'But it did not work out the way I wished,' Seraphina said sulkily.

'We misjudged him. I know you don't want to hear it, but it is the truth. There is more to this man of yours than at first met the eye. We have not got to the bottom of him yet, and until we do, you will not be able to play him as you wish.'

'Humph!' Seraphina growled, but she knew that her old nurse was right. She had thought Lord Brandon was like her cousin Harry. Allow him her body, pleasure him with her lips, and he would be hers to do with what she liked, for as long as she liked. Harry was putty in her fingers, but not his lordship, who had not even given her the chance to show what she could do to a man like him.

Seraphina wriggled on her stool. She let out a long, low breath, her breasts rising and falling, as she thought of what and how she could show him. Her eyes strayed to the door. If only he were to walk in now …

'You could do such things he would think he was transported to paradise,' Megan whispered in her ear. 'But it won't happen if you do nothing but sit here in a great big grump.' And she gave Seraphina a slap on her naked rump.

'You are right, Megan. I will go to him. Not to beg his pardon, or to give any reason or explanation for what he imagined he saw, but,' she licked her tongue over her lips and lowered her voice to a low purr, 'to show him what he is missing.'

'That's my lady!' Megan clapped her hands and bustled away to fetch water and clean towels, while Seraphina sat by the glowing embers of the fire and plotted her next move.

The scarlet dress fitted closely round her waist, the bodice so tightly laced that her breasts were forced upwards, spilling over the silk that scarcely skimmed the top of her nipples. To make it even more tantalising, a scarf of lace so fine as to be almost transparent was fastened around her shoulders, veiling but not hiding the curve and swell of her breasts.

Her skirts billowed out over her hips, the silk swishing suggestively as she walked. She wore high-heeled shoes with silver buckles. Her hair was swept up on the top of her head, exposing the creamy column of her neck, and she hung one pearl earring in her ear.

'Now his lordship's necklace to finish the picture,' Megan said, going over to the chest.

'No. Not yet. He would see it as a sign of the submission I am not prepared to make, now or ever. The Lady of Witchcraven bows before no man. The Goddess would not allow it.'

'Indeed she would not,' Megan nodded. 'Let me look at you. You are as ripe as a peach for the taking, but noble as the Lady herself would wish you to be. The Goddess grant you speed and success.'

The old woman traced a sign of blessing in the air. Then, digging Seraphina in the ribs, she chortled, 'Be sure to come back and tell me all about it. How he begged for you to do it again and again.' Her hips swayed suggestively. 'How you rode him till your cunt was sore and he was spent. Make him your slave, my lady. Your adoring follower till death or the Goddess tear you apart. Now go, and don't hold back. Remember you have the power.'

Outside, at the front of the house, the stable boy held Moonlight, the stallion's coat gleaming sliver white in the chill winter sun. For a moment Seraphina wondered if her own wishes had conjured him up, then she realised that Megan must have arranged this before she came up with the hot water. The boy, his eye riveted on the flash of ankle she allowed him, held her stirrup as she mounted.

Seraphina rode slowly to the top of the ridge overlooking the valley that sheltered her beloved Witchcraven. When she reached the top she reined in her mount. Sat high in her saddle, the powerfully-muscled horse beneath her thighs, she looked down at the house, brooding and mysterious under its low slate roof. This was where she and the daughter she would bear belonged; and to make sure of that she would do whatever she must.

'I have the power and the blessing of the Goddess herself. I cannot fail in what I set out to do, and I will not,' Seraphina vowed, her breath rising into the icy air. Then, spurring on Moonlight, she let him have his head in a wild gallop over the uplands.

They rode like the wind, past the hollow where she had initiated Harry into the joys of her body, past the stone circle and its latent power and over wide swathes of heather until at last they dipped down into a wide valley.

The landscape here was tamer. A river meandered between wide banks, and the ground beneath the stallion's feet was soft with grass. Trees grew on the sides of the hills and lined the drive that led up to Brandon Hall.

The house itself was surrounded by immaculately kept lawns, and in front of it was a lake. At one end there was a small classical temple, at the other the white shape of the Hall. Its blank windows staring out at the silver water, it looked forbidding and lacking in life.

Seraphina shuddered as she reined Moonlight in before the sweep of stone steps that led to the front doors. How could anyone bear to live here? The very thought of stepping through those glazed doors made her want to turn her horse's head and gallop home to the warmth and familiarity of Witchcraven as fast as she could. On the other hand, Witchcraven would not last for very much longer without Brandon Hall and all its wealth, so she must do what she had come to do. Forcing a smile to her lips, she let the footman help her dismount. Then, holding her head high, she swept in through the front door.

'My lady, I am afraid nothing is prepared. We did not expect you. His lordship did not say…' the butler stammered.

Seraphina suppressed a frown. This was not the welcome she had imagined. 'And his lordship is where?' She turned her full gaze on the embarrassed servant.

'His lordship is not at home,' came a voice from the top of the stairs.

Seraphina looked up and saw a voluptuous woman in a blue silk gown. Her fair hair was tied on the top of her head, except for a couple of ringlets that had been arranged so that they fell over her billowing breasts. An earring of sapphires and diamonds hung from one ear and there was a small pendant of the same stones around her neck. Her skin was white as milk, her lips red, but without the use of paint.

Who is this creature? Seraphina wondered. As far as she knew, Lord Brandon had no sister or cousin who lived with him. But the woman was obviously no servant. The way she walked down the staircase as if she were the mistress of the place clearly showed that. She had not, however, introduced herself, so Seraphina decided that until she did so, she would treat her as the housekeeper.

Seraphina clenched her fists, then unclenched them as the woman reached the hall. 'I will wait in my sitting room until his lordship returns,' she said coolly.

The woman looked at her, and there was both surprise and admiration in her eyes. 'Of course, my lady,' she said. 'If you will come this way, I will show you into the blue boudoir.'

She knows who I am, but she was not expecting me. None of the servants was. What has he told them? Has he said I am some mad creature that has to be shut away in a remote manor house? Or has he said that I have displeased him in some way and he is punishing me? No. Not even Brandon with all his arrogance would do that. Or would he? The slight sliver of doubt made her heart beat faster, the palms of her hands feel hot.

'Take her ladyship's cloak,' the woman said to one of

the footmen.

Seraphina slipped the cloak from her shoulders, then followed the woman, who led her, not as she had expected into a room on the ground floor, but back up the marble staircase.

At the top, the corridor ran along three sides of the entrance hall, which was covered by a glazed dome so that the winter light streamed in through the glass. Although it was bright and airy, there was a cold, impersonal feeling about the place. Here there was nothing warm and passionate; everything was formal and controlled. Quite different from the woman who led her along the corridor, Seraphina thought appraisingly. She radiated an animal warmth. There was something about the swing of her hips, the silky softness of her hair, the firm rise and fall of her breasts, that invited you to touch and feel and stroke.

'My lady's boudoir. You can wait in here.'

The woman opened a door and stood aside as Seraphina swept past her with a deliberately insulting turn of her head and swish of her skirts. She would have to put this trollop well and truly in her place. Whatever that was. Although, the more she thought about it, the more convinced she was that this woman was the reason why she herself had been left at Witchcraven. Her husband must have thought that to keep his mistress at Brandon Hall while his wife languished at Witchcraven was the perfect revenge. What he did not know, and what she had no intention of telling him, was that she preferred Witchcraven, with its simple ways, to this vast mausoleum of a place. Since what he had done could not hurt her, she would use it to her advantage.

Seraphina suppressed a smile and looked around her. The room in which she found herself was rightly called the blue boudoir. The walls were covered in blue silk. The curtains, which were lavishly draped and swagged, were of damask in the same colour and fringed with silver. A silver-framed mirror hung over the white marble fireplace, where a fire burned brightly. The carpet was woven with tiny flowers that looked as though they had been spilled onto a blue sky, while on the ceiling plump white clouds had been painted onto an azure background.

A chaise longue, lavishly heaped with silken pillows, stood by the window. There were two comfortable chairs either side of the hearth and another smaller sofa at the foot of the bed. The bed itself had been extravagantly dressed with flowing curtains and satin coverlets of every shade of blue, from the deep, dark navy of almost-night to the searing blue of a brilliant summer's day. The pillows were plump and inviting, but what caught Seraphina's eye was the silver moon that hung on a slender chain above the bedhead.

'Some of the older servants call this the moon chamber,' the woman said, following her glance. 'A fitting room for the mistress of this house,' she added when Seraphina did not reply.

'Indeed,' Seraphina said as coolly as she could, but her eyes were drawn again to the symbol of the Goddess.

'This is always her ladyship's private sitting room. No-one comes here unless invited,' the woman continued. Looking down, her lashes swept the curve of her cheek and she flushed slightly, sending a delightful pink from her face down her neck and over her breasts and into the cleavage between them.

Seraphina moved her weight from one leg to another, swaying her hips as she did so. The tip of her tongue explored her bottom lip as something about the husky tone of the woman's voice stirred her.

'Not even his lordship?' Seraphina lowered her voice to match the tone of her companion's.

'Not even he,' the woman murmured. She cast a swift glance upwards, and Seraphina saw the widening of her pupils, the sudden quick in-drawing of breath, before she looked down again.

'You however seem very familiar with this room. You brought me here as if you had the right.'

'I have no right. It is for the mistress of Brandon Hall only.'

'Mistress.' Seraphina tossed her head. 'Is that what you are?'

'No, my lady. You are the mistress here.'

'Yet you show me around as if this were your house.'

'I live here, it is true.'

'As his lordship's whore!' Striking as swiftly as a snake, Seraphina seized the woman by the wrist and pulled her close. 'And as his lordship's whore you have no right in this room. You have no right in this house. It is mine!'

Releasing her grip, she flung the woman from her. The woman fell half on the floor, half on the bed, and as she did so her dress slid from her shoulders, revealing her naked breasts.

'Whatever you may think, I am no whore.' Without adjusting her dress, the woman got to her feet.

'Oh no? Then what are you doing living here with my husband, taking the place that rightfully belongs to me?'

The woman flushed and, lifting her head, said, 'I am Artemisia Fitzgerald, Lord Brandon's mistress. No, do not be angry, at least until I have finished. I have been with George Brandon since he was a young lad. I have taught him much, though not all, of what he knows. He is a strong and lusty lover. You should and you will be grateful to me.'

Grateful to her! Seraphina's temper bubbled. What had this floozie, this dolly mop, to teach her? She had been initiated into the cult of the Goddess, and it was she, Seraphina, who could teach this miserable piece of skirt a thing or two.

'You think so!' she hissed. 'Let me tell you, there is nothing that you could teach either of us of the arts of love, now or ever.'

'If that is so, then why did he return from his marriage bed so unsatisfied? Believe me, my lady, my very cunt aches from the drumming I have since been given.'

'Bitch!' Seraphina hissed. Raising her arm, she aimed a blow at Artemisia's face, but the other woman was quicker than she expected and grabbed hold of her wrist.

'Oh no you don't. You may be angry with me, but from all accounts you have only yourself to blame.'

'No,' Seraphina snarled, and brought her leg up hard between Artemisia's legs. The other woman screamed and fell backwards onto the bed. Seraphina's nails flexed as she leapt up over her. 'Brandon's mistress, are you? By the time I've finished tearing your face to pieces he'll have you thrown out the door. Then see who you'll be teaching what.'

She brought down her hand, and Artemisia turned her head and raised the whole of her body in a desperate attempt to escape the sharpness of her nails. The move threw Seraphina off balance and she tumbled down onto the bed beside her. Instantly Artemisia seized her advantage. Rolling Seraphina over onto her back, she straddled her. Holding her firmly between her legs, she leaned forward and clamped her hands to the bed. As she did so, her breasts grazed Seraphina's chest. At the touch of skin on skin, Artemisia's nipples visibly hardened. She lowered her head, and Seraphina struggled violently, afraid of the damage teeth could do to her face; but prone on her back, she was no match for the other woman. As Artemisia's mouth descended, Seraphina shut her eyes and sent up a desperate prayer to the Goddess. She could feel the warmth of Artemisia's breath, smell her scent of jasmine and spice, feel the full softness of the other woman's lips on hers, the swift thrust of her tongue as it darted in, then withdrew.

'Do not, do not ever tell me that you cannot learn something new from one who is an expert in the art of pleasure,' she murmured.

'Never,' Seraphina gasped, though every nerve in her body longed to open herself up to what was offered, to take those little hard pink buds into her mouth, to open her lips to that probing tongue, her legs …

'Never?' Artemisia murmured, her lips moving down Seraphina's neck. Inch by delicious inch, kisses soft as feathers gathered in intensity until at last her tongue lapped at the cleft between Seraphina's breasts. 'Shall I cease now?' she whispered. 'Is this enough for our first lesson?'

'No, please, don't stop.' Seraphina tried to move her hand, and with a low, throaty laugh Artemisia released her grip so that she could push away the tight band of her bodice and let her breasts fall free.

'A fine pair, my lady. Firm and ripe as autumn plums.' Artemisia's lips fastened on one of Seraphina's nipples and, as her teeth tightened, Seraphina bucked in a sudden shock of pleasure. 'Oh, we can do better than that. Much better.' Artemisia's hand moved downwards, her fingers deftly undoing Seraphina's laces until she was naked from the waist down.

'Oh!' Seraphina cried, and her body was pressed to the silken covers as breast lay upon breast. 'Oh!' she cried again as Artemisia's hand reached between her legs. The feel of the other woman's fingers through the silk of her petticoats inflamed her. Her cunt, already moist, began to flow, and she moaned with pleasure as the fingers toyed with her mound. Her thighs fell open, and Artemisia bent her head and kissed her neck. Seraphina moved her shoulders, stretching her body out over the bed. If she were a cat, she would have purred. There was no hurry, no race to orgasm. This was pure enjoyment given and received. She lifted her head and kissed Artemisia fully on the lips. She tasted chocolate and wine, breathed in the other woman's perfume and the muskiness of her arousal.

Artemisia turned on her side, so that they were lying alongside each other. She still had her hand on Seraphina's cunt, but now Seraphina moved her own hand downwards to the dip between the other woman's legs. 'Let me,' she murmured. 'Let me feel you too.'

'Mmm,' Artemisia sighed. She lifted her hips a little and wriggled so that her skirts rose and, billowing up around her hips, revealed her silk stockings and above them the firm column of her white thighs and the golden thatch of her pubic hair. Seraphina let her fingers linger among the curls.

Artemisia's stroking intensified, and as the rhythm quickened Seraphina became more and more inflamed. No longer content to dally on the outside, she was sliding her forefinger in between the hotness of Artemisia's open labia when …

'What have we here, pray?'

Both women heard his footsteps, but neither looked

up until he stood at the end of the bed.

'Why, lessons in love, my lord.' Flushed and panting, Artemisia pushed Seraphina gently onto her back and sat up. Her skin glowed, her nipples were pink and hard, her golden hair tumbled over her shoulders. Running her tongue over her lips, she crawled cat-like to the end of the bed, lifted her head and licked out her tongue at the erection visible in the potent swell of Lord Brandon's britches. 'Though I can see you need none of my teaching.' Sinking back on her heels, she watched as he unbuttoned himself. 'My lord?' She glanced at him sideways, daring him to choose between herself and Seraphina, who lay prone on the bed, not sure what move to make.

'Artemisia,' he murmured, 'turn over.'

'Like this?' She turned on all fours and presented the round globes of her buttocks.

'Yes.' In one sharp movement he thrust inside her.

'My lord,' she cried out, and in the moment Seraphina saw that, she came. As her orgasm rippled through her, Brandon's eye caught hers. His lips curved into a half smile, and he climaxed with a deliberation that stole away her breath.

Withdrawing, he patted his mistress's behind, in a gesture both playful and affectionate, which was more hurtful than anything else he could have done. He buttoned himself up, stretched, and said, 'Get dressed, ladies, and send for tea.'

'My lord.' Artemisia scrambled from the bed. She laced up her bodice, went to the silver-framed mirror, and with an easy, practiced gesture tied up her hair.

Seraphina was clumsier. Hurt beyond anything she could have imagined, at the same time she was brimming with fury as she stumbled from the bed. Her fingers seemed to have turned into elephant trunks, her laces into ropes greased with lard, and however hard she tried, she could not fit them into the right holes.

Artemisia, looking as neat and tidy as she had when she first appeared at the top of the staircase, regarded Seraphina with some amusement. 'Do you need some help?'

'No,' Seraphina said between gritted teeth.

'Oh, for God's sake lace her up,' Brandon said carelessly. 'I'm parched, and I'm sure my lady would prefer it if the servants did not see her in this state.'

'My lord, you would not be so cruel.' Artemisia turned quickly to Seraphina and fastened up her dress. 'Do not take it so hard,' she murmured as she rearranged the lace around her shoulders. 'Whatever he thinks you have done, you have paid for it. And I –' She moved closer and put her arm around Seraphina's waist. 'I greatly enjoyed our encounter.' She kissed her quickly and kindly, then glided elegantly away. 'I shall ring for tea, if that is what you wish, my lady,' she said, looking directly at Seraphina.

What was she to do? Sit down and drink a civilised cup of tea with her husband and his mistress, or storm out in righteous fury? Seraphina lowered her eyes, avoiding both of them as she considered her options. Her anger against Brandon was limitless; if she could, she would have done him the worst possible injury she could inflict. What she felt about Artemisia however was different. On the one hand, the woman had obviously used her; on the other, what had happened between them had been more than pleasurable, and that final whispered message suggested that Artemisia had some sympathy for her. Then again, Artemisia was Brandon's mistress, and she rather than Seraphina was living with him at Brandon Hall. Nor was there any hint that the situation was going to change. Unless she was expected to join them, when her husband decided it was time for her to leave Witchcraven and move into his house ...

It was obvious that Lord Brandon's intention was to be in control of both women. He also expected both of them to do as he wanted. That was something Seraphina was not prepared to accept.

He had got his revenge for what she had done with Harry on their wedding night. That she had to concede. So be it. She was still not going to give in to him. If he wanted her as his wife, then he would have to come begging; and if that took until the seas ran dry, then that was his misfortune. Just so long as they stayed married. And there were no grounds for him to put her aside. Their marriage had been consummated. Witchcraven was now safe, so she could do as she liked. She had Harry, a pleasing if not overwhelming lover. When she tired of him there would be others. And there were always the rituals of the Goddess to look forward too. Remembering her first night at the stones, the lustiness of the horned man, Seraphina half closed her eyes and gave a small sigh.

Hearing the breath leave her lips, Artemisia gave her a brief smile, one that died quickly on her lips as Lord Brandon looked at his wife. Even from under her lowered lashes, Seraphina saw the sudden fleeting glimpse of pain on his face, which was quickly followed by the raising of an eyebrow, the sneering curl of a lip.

It was enough. Lord Brandon, in spite of the despicable way in which he treated her, was vulnerable. Was it her youth and beauty? Seraphina straightened her back and thrust out her breasts, holding her head proudly and turning it slowly and disdainfully so that he could see the graceful column of her neck, the firm line of her chin, the curve of her cheek, the scarlet redness of her lips, which she enhanced by a swift lick of her tongue. She was beautiful and she was desirable; she could see that in her reflection in the silver-framed mirror.

There was however something else that bound him to her. He may have taken her, he may have scorned her, but there was something he had not taken from her, and he knew it. In spite of all his thrusting and sneering, the deepest part of her was hidden from him. That she had given freely to the horned man on the altar of the Goddess that night. Her midnight lover had had from her the very core of her being, where lust, desire and gentleness merged, where it was as satisfying to lie in a man's arms as to come all over him. To feel both part of him and yet separate. In control and controlled. Dominant and submissive.

She had been given a true gift from the Goddess that night. In a rare moment of humility, Seraphina bent her head and murmured a quick prayer of thanks. As her lips framed the ancient words, Brandon gave her a questioning glance.

'My lady?' he prompted.

Choosing to ignore the unspoken question, Seraphina made a quick decision. 'I am afraid I will not stay for tea, my lord,' she said coolly. She turned to Artemisia. 'Perhaps another time.' She nodded her head and swept out of the room.

The great marble staircase seemed endless as she walked down it. Portraits of long dead Brandons stared down at her, their eyes seeming to pierce through her flesh. In the entrance hall two footmen stood, stiff-backed, their eyes averted. They would not dare to say anything, but she knew that they would be wondering why his lordship's new wife was leaving so quickly.

Too bad, she told herself. *Let them think what they like. Let them gossip and spread their rumours. None of it will touch me. I am the Lady of Witchcraven. Those who matter to me, those who worship the Goddess as I do, will know why I act as I do. They will rejoice to see their Lady in the ascendant. Living in her own house, taking part in the ancient mysteries and treating her husband as the Ladies of Witchcraven have done throughout the centuries, as a tool for her own using.*

Reaching the bottom of the staircase, she ordered one of the footmen to send for her horse. His face impassive, the man bowed and hurried to do as she said, after first suggesting that she might like to wait in the library while the stallion was being saddled.

Although she wanted nothing more than to jump onto Moonlight's back straightaway and ride home as fast as she could, Seraphina was glad to take up this suggestion. She knew that in her current state of suppressed fury and cold determination she would not be able to keep still, and if she paced up and down the marble entrance hall, then his lordship's servants would see her agitation. They did not matter, but word might get back to Brandon, for any one of these blank-faced lackeys might be questioned by his master about what he had seen. Even worse would be if Artemisia, or Brandon himself, saw her.

Artemisia was clearly a clever and worldly woman. She would choose what she told her lover, and would make sure it was something that would keep him at her side. She had everything she could want here at Brandon Hall, and she was never going to risk losing that. Besides, Seraphina suspected that with Artemisia, more than money was at stake. The older woman cared deeply for Lord Brandon and was no doubt delighted that his new wife was causing him so much trouble. As for Brandon himself, Seraphina had to be cold and distant with him, until she had made up her mind what she was going to do next to bring her arrogant husband to heel.

The library at Brandon Hall took up the whole of one side of the main building. There were bookcases from floor to ceiling, all filled to the brim with leather-bound books. Rows of long windows looked out on the front of the house, where a breeze ruffled the smooth waters of the lake and sent puffs of cloud scurrying over a rapidly greying sky. The weather was turning, and it seemed that snow was on the way …

Seraphina shook her head resolutely. Even if it snowed up to very rooftops it would not stop her from returning to Witchcraven. Being trapped in this soulless place was a prospect she could not bear. She would rather risk her neck riding home than stay safe where Lord Brandon and his mistress could gloat over her.

She looked out of the window again. If she left soon, she thought, she would make it back without too much difficulty. She had often ridden over the moors in bad weather. Moonlight was surefooted and strong, and if the snow was too bad there were places she knew where she could shelter until the worst of the storm passed.

Her stomach tightened with anxiety, and to distract herself she went over to the shelves and looked at the ranks of books. From what she could see, as she paced up and down the long room, most were boring tomes, some in Latin and other foreign languages; but in a secluded bay she found something much more interesting.

It was the binding that first caught her eye: sapphire blue leather embossed in silver. It reminded her of the blue boudoir that belonged to the mistress of Brandon Hall. Looking more closely, however, she recognised the shape of the pentangle on the cover. To her surprise, she had found a book on the occult arts. Carefully, almost religiously, she took it from the shelf and, carrying it over to a low chair, sat down and began to turn the pages.

The book described a number of magical rituals. Some she recognised, others were new to her. The ones that had come from the mystical practices of the Ancient Egyptians were the most interesting, and she would have immersed herself in studying them had she not been aware that at any moment she might be interrupted by the footman returning to say that her horse had been saddled and was waiting for her to ride away. So, after a tantalising glimpse and a promise to herself that one day she would learn everything this book had to teach her, she slipped it back into its place on the shelf. As she did so, she saw that it was not the only book in this part of the library that dealt with the magic arts. The whole of this section was devoted to the subject. Seraphina stood in front of the bookcase and frowned. What were these books doing there? They were not for the casual reader, but for the adept in magic and magical practices. Was there more to Brandon Hall than met the eye? If so, why had no-one told her? Megan had said nothing, nor had she ever heard any rumours. So either the secrets of the Brandons were well kept, or this collection of arcana was no more than the strange hobby of some past lord – for there was nothing about the current holder of the title to suggest that he had any interest in such matters. Except for the way in which he had known about Harry and what had passed on their wedding night ...

Seraphina shook her head. Either that had been a

lucky guess or Megan had been mistaken about the strength of the sleeping draught she had put into the wine. She was sure her husband could not possess psychic powers, because if he did, she would know. Wouldn't she?

She was still puzzling over this when the footman entered and told her that Midnight was ready for her. 'The weather however is worsening, my lady, and his lordship wishes me to inform you that if you would care to stay, he will have your room made ready for you.'

My room! Seraphina thought bitterly. *What room is that likely to be? Some inferior bedroom at the back of the house, while his lordship and his whore disport themselves in the best chamber – which is my right!*

The thought of Artemisia and her husband pleasuring each other was not what made Seraphina angry. It was Brandon's treatment of her, not what he was doing with his mistress, that infuriated her almost beyond reason. In a different world, in a different situation, she would be more than willing to share her bed and her man with the other woman.

At the thought of Artemisia's fair loveliness, and especially the blonde curls between her thighs, Seraphina ran her tongue over her lower lip and smiled. So it was that when she followed the footman out into the hall, and waited while he slipped her cloak over her shoulders, she was in a happy state of semi-arousal, and a fleeting glimpse of a black-coated figure glowering down at her from the top of the staircase did nothing to upset her.

Nodding her head serenely at the servant, she put up her hood and stepped out into the wild wind.

10

Moonlight greeted her with an excited whinny, and without waiting to be helped, Seraphina leapt onto his back. She knew she was being watched, by the footmen and the groom, Brandon too and Artemisia. She could sense it. Let them think of her what they wanted. She was no delicate lady who could do nothing for herself. She was wild and she was free. Her own woman with her own powers. Brandon might think that he was punishing her by not formally accepting her as the mistress of his house, so how furious would he be if he knew that in fact he was giving her the freedom she craved?

The wind caught Seraphina's cloak, tearing it from her head and loosening her hair so that it flew out behind her as she urged Moonlight into a gallop down the long, tree-lined drive. Above their heads branches waved wildly, spurring them on, so that it was not long before they had left the confines of the park behind them and were climbing the steep upland path.

The higher they went, the wilder the wind. It roared and swirled around them, screeching like a lost soul across the bleak expanse of the moorland and bringing with it the first of the snow. The flakes fell slowly from the clouds, caught in a frozen dance as they tumbled to earth. Careful of Moonlight's safety, Seraphina reined him in. For all that she despised Lord Greville, she was his daughter, and she would never knowingly put any animal of hers in harm's way. She slowed his pace to a trot and then a walk, for the ground here could be treacherous, with sudden unseen dips and clefts that could easily turn a horse's hoof.

As they traversed the top of the ridge, the shape of the stone circle loomed out of the whiteness of the falling snow. In a landscape where earth and sky appeared to merge into one, it did indeed look like the Devil's Crown – the name ignorant villagers gave it. Seraphina threw back her head and laughed. There was only one devil here, and he wore a black coat and lived not up on this wild moorland, but in the opulence and comfort of Brandon Hall.

The stones reminded her that this was a temple to the Goddess, and that she was one of Her priestesses and should be treated with reverence and respect, not as if she were a worthless scullery maid. Her anger soared, and she swore that she would have her revenge. Never again would Lord Brandon humiliate her, or any other woman. She would cast a spell to deny him the pleasure of her body, or anyone else's – girl, woman, man or boy. He would become impotent, his cock limp and flabby, dangling useless between his thighs. However desperately he tried, whatever potions he took, it would never rise again, not even in his dreams.

'Come on, boy.' She dug her heels into Moonlight's side, urging him on toward the stone circle. The closer they got, the more reluctant the horse became, but Seraphina did not hurry him. Very soon she would dismount and leave him to wait until she returned. He would not leave her, but neither would he enter the circle. No horse she had owned ever would. It was as if they sensed the holiness of the place and were content to wait on the periphery while their rider worshiped their Goddess.

'Good boy.' Seraphina slid from the stallion's back. She leaned against his side and stroked his neck to comfort and reassure him. He lowered his head and she whispered in his ear that she would come back, that she was safe and all he had to do was to keep as far out of the wind as he could and wait patiently until she returned. When she was sure that the stallion understood, she gave him a final pat and set off down the avenue of stones toward the altar at the centre of the circle.

Although the wind and snow raged around them, the moment she stepped into the shelter of the stones it was as if the storm no longer existed. It was so still and silent that she could hear her own breath, quick and eager, as she made her way down the long line of stones. There was no snow here either. It was as if an invisible canopy was stretched over the circle, protecting it and all who entered from the violence of the tempest. The air was warmer too and sweeter.

The stillness and the silence calmed Seraphina's anger. Her pace slowed, and the closer she got to the centre, the more peaceful she felt. However hard she fought to keep them, all thoughts of revenge slid from her mind. She had come to cast a spell, but instead she herself was being put under an enchantment.

Reaching the altar stone, she raised her arms to the sky. Above her head the clouds parted and a pale, silvery sun sailed into view. A single ray fell like a spear to the centre of the altar stone. Seraphina raised her face to its warmth. Its heat ran through her, and she slid the cloak from her shoulders. Still she burned. Unlacing her dress, she let it fall to the ground, then her corset, and finally her petticoats drifted down her legs like the snow that was rapidly covering the tops of the nearby hills. Seraphina however felt no cold. Her whole body pulsed with a gentle heat. Her skin was smooth, her hair silky against her back, and she was filled with a sense of joy and rightness that she had never felt in her life before. This was where she belonged. Here, naked as the day she was born, she was both no more than a small fragment of all living beings and at the same time part of a greater eternal whole.

Falling to her knees, she prayed to the Goddess. 'Maiden, Mother, Crone, bless me and help me to do Thy will.'

A cloud covered the sun and shrouded the stones in darkness. It was as if time itself had stopped. Then, gradually, she was aware of a faint silver light piercing the gloom. The stones appeared to be glowing; silver, then blue, they pulsated with a light that grew stronger and stronger, focusing on the altar stone, gathering shape and solidity until at last Seraphina could make out the figure of a woman. The figure was indistinct, almost transparent, but she could see that she was dressed in a white robe, with a silver rope about her waist. Her long hair fell over her shoulders and was held back from her face by a silver circlet from which rose the shape of the crescent moon. Her face and limbs shimmered so intensely that Seraphina could not look and was forced to cover her head with her arms.

Pressing her face against the smooth surface of the stone, Seraphina felt the touch of a hand on her shoulder.

Light and insubstantial as a passing breeze, it was both powerful and soothing. She felt she could do anything; that all things were possible to her. But even though she had this power, she understood that there was nothing that she need do.

'To have what you desire, you must do as I desire,' came a voice as sweet and smooth as honey. The hand rested on her shoulder again, then it was gone. Without daring to look, Seraphina felt the presence of the Goddess retreat. Like a child suddenly deprived of her mother, she was about to give way to tears when another voice, this time a male one, said:

'Do not weep. She has not gone. She is still here. She is all around us. If you wish to find her, then all you must do is as she has commanded.'

'But …' Seraphina began, then stopped as a hand curved round her breast. A head lowered and lips nuzzled at the back of her neck, sending tremors of electricity through her veins. She leaned back against the man's firmly muscled body, breathed in his scent. 'It's you,' she murmured.

He did not reply. His other hand slid around her breast and he pulled her up, sliding her along his body, so that she felt the powerful muscles of his thighs, the hardness of his prick against her buttocks, the firmness of his chest.

Once on her feet she let him hold her, almost unwilling to turn around in case this was nothing but a vision sent by the Goddess. For how could the horned man, the lover of her dreams, the priest of the midnight ritual, be here at the stone circle? Where had he come from? Or had he too been summoned in some mysterious way by the Goddess herself?

'Shhh.' As if he knew the questions she dare not ask,

he put his finger on her lips. 'We are here, that is all you need to know,' he said, and slowly he turned her round to face him.

He stood silhouetted against the whiteness of the sky. The horns of his mask rose above his head. He wore a torque around his neck, but apart from that he was completely naked. Seraphina breathed in and let herself sway toward him. He however stepped back a pace. Swept by a feeling of rejection, she quickly became tearful, but he took her hand and, in a gesture of respect, raised it to his lips.

'My lady,' he murmured, and as they stood there hand in hand, the sun broke free of the clouds and shone down onto them.

They stood in the light as solemnly as if they were being wed, then he lifted her up and gently laid her on the altar stone. Warmed by the mysterious light, softened by some mystic power, Seraphina was held in its embrace. She stretched out her arms, lifting her breasts, pert and firm in invitation. He positioned himself above her, his erection grazing her belly as he lowered his head and curled his tongue around her nipple. First the right breast, then the left, he licked and sucked tenderly at first, then fiercer, harder, sending judders of pleasure through her body.

She was on the cusp, about to come, but she held back, not wanting this lovemaking to end.

'I am ready for you, so ready,' she murmured. 'But I think we do not want to hurry.'

As if he knew what she had in mind, he turned onto his side. Her hand found his nipple, her fingers fastened round it, teasing and pinching, until finally she lowered her head and drew it into her mouth. Her tongue curled around it, sucking gently, and he shuddered with pleasure. For a moment she was afraid she had gone too fast and he would not be able to hold back, and she lifted her head. Her eyes caught his through the mask, and he smiled.

'I too do not want to hurry,' he said. He turned her onto her back and nuzzled at the soft curve of her belly, then worked his way down until reaching her bush. He stopped and looked at her. 'Now?'

'Not yet,' she sighed luxuriously, savouring the build-up of pleasure, but willing to delay it. 'My turn.'

He stretched himself out on the stone and she took his cock in her hand, her fingers gliding over it, down and down, until she reached the bottom of the shaft, when she curled her fingers around his balls and bent her head.

The air between them vibrated. They were both on the edge of orgasm. Her eyes again met his, dark and mysterious behind his mask. He moved his buttocks against the stone, thrusting them upwards in an involuntary gesture, inviting her yet not insisting.

Seraphina did not take him in her mouth. Moving a little to the side, she knelt and opened her legs, displaying the scarlet openness of her cunt, the proud lift of her clitoris. He slid his finger into her cleft. His thumb pressed against her button. Her breath quickened, her hips moved in response to the tightening and loosening within. It would be so easy, so good to let herself go, but she did not. Instead she took hold of his wrist and he stopped.

Once again their eyes met. There was no need to speak. The time had come. Seraphina lay back on the stone, he lay above her. His lips on hers were an affirmation of everything that had not been spoken but was understood between them. She was his, he was hers.

There was no dominance, no submission. Their pleasure was shared, was mutual. Her satisfaction was as important to him as his own; she cared as much for his joy and pleasure as she did for hers.

He thrust into her slowly. She gave a cry and let herself close around him. For a moment they held that position, then his pace quickened, and hers with it. Faster, stronger, harder he thrust, and as he moved inside her, his rhythm became hers. Every nerve in her body responded, the pleasure rippled through her, growing in intensity, and her climax grew closer and closer.

She was aware of nothing but him, the hardness inside her that was carrying her away, transporting her to a place she had never been before, to a state where nothing mattered but the two of them and this unending wave of utter and complete pleasure that was sweeping through her. Carried out of herself, she dissolved, became totally, utterly at one with him, and then beyond, so that the two of them no longer existed as one but were part of the universe, the wholeness of creation. Stars danced and planets whirled. The universe spun and took them with it.

The wave reached its height and then slowly, slowly ebbed away. There was no sudden withdrawal; it was as if they were still one. There was no distance between them. His arms were around her, hers were around him. They breathed in each other's scent, their hearts beat with the same pulse, their breath came in the same moment. They were truly two halves of one whole.

They did not speak of love. There was no need; there were no words for what they had been given.

Seraphina did not want to move. She wanted to stay where she was forever. She put her hand up to touch his face, stroke his cheek, her fingers moving up toward the mask that he wore.

'No.' The word broke the spell. His arms still held her close, his heart still beat against hers, but now they were two separate beings again. They lay together for a while, satisfied and content, enjoying each other's warmth, until with a final kiss he slid his arms from around her. She tried to hold him, but he was too quick. One moment he was with her, the next he was standing at the side of the stone. The horned mask loomed above her. Tall, broad-shouldered, slim-hipped, his figure was outlined against the whirling snow, and then he was gone, merging into the shadow of the stones as if he was as unsubstantial as a dream.

Seraphina closed her eyes and stretched slowly. Every cell of her body was satisfied. She had never been loved, or had loved, like this. It was truly a gift from the Goddess. It was also a lesson. But a lesson for what?

There was no time to puzzle that out. Opening her eyes, she saw that beyond the stones the storm was at its height. The light was fading, the day was closing in. It was time to leave if she wanted to reach Witchcraven before the snow became too deep for Moonlight.

She found her clothes, dressed quickly and, after a quick prayer of thanks, hurried down the avenue of stones to where the horse had found a sheltered spot out of the worst of the storm. She patted his neck and he nuzzled her as if he was glad to see her but had not been worried by her absence. She leapt onto his back and they rode out into the blizzard.

The wind caught at her cloak, almost ripping it off her shoulders, and she had to lean low in the saddle as Moonlight fought his way along the ridge. Her skin was raw from the cold, her fingers numb on the reins. There were drops of ice on the horse's mane, and she could feel the strain in his muscles as he searched out firm ground. With every hoof beat the snow thickened, until they were riding into a whirling white blanket.

Then, just as she was wondering if they should find somewhere to shelter and wait out the worst of the storm, the path began to dip and, peering down into the valley, Seraphina thought she could see the faint glimmer of lights. The horse too sensed that they were reaching the end of their journey, and he began to move more confidently.

'My lady, where have you been?' the stable boy cried as he came running to hold Moonlight's reins. 'We were going to send out men with lanterns to search for you.'

'Then they would surely have got lost on the uplands,' Seraphina laughed, sliding down from the horse's back without waiting to be helped. 'Rub him down and feed him well.' She dropped a kiss on the horse's nose and hurried into the warmth of house.

11

A fire roared in the hearth. In front of it steamed a bath of hot water, filling the bedroom with the sleepy scent of lavender. Seraphina yawned and let her clothes slip from her shoulders. Naked, she could still smell him on her skin, but as she breathed in, her vision blurred. The room spun. She felt Megan's hand steadying her, helping her into the hot water, then she lay back and closed her eyes.

Her limbs grew loose and heavy, her breathing slowed. She was sliding into sleep when Megan's voice broke through the haze.

'How was your handsome husband when you left him? Was he panting for more? Or did you leave him satisfied?'

'I didn't do it.' Seraphina sat up, scattering drops of water all over the old woman.

'More fool you.' Megan clicked her tongue.

'I don't mean that,' Seraphina cried impatiently. 'I went to the stones to curse him, but I did not, I could not do it. Why, Megan, why?'

'You belong to Lord Brandon. You are his. That is why you could not bring yourself to harm him.'

Megan held out the towel that had been airing by the fire, and as Seraphina stepped out of the bath, she wrapped it around her. The towel was warm, but Seraphina shuddered.

'I belong to no-one,' she muttered. 'I am my own woman. You have always said so.'

'And so it is and always shall be,' Megan said. 'But you are bound together, man and woman.'

'Never. I did not choose him. He has humiliated me, and for that I will have my revenge.'

Megan clicked her tongue and shook her head sadly. 'When will you ever learn? This fighting is not the way. You must be together, my little one.'

'We will be, if and when he does my will. In the meantime, let him whistle for me.'

'No good will come of this,' Megan said.

'I will have what I desire.'

'And you will pay for it.'

'Then let it be,' Seraphina said lightly. The Goddess had told her she must follow her desire. Why then did she feel this sudden chill? Why did her limbs ache and her head throb?

'Little one, you are not well.' Megan helped her sit down. Taking another towel, she dried her limbs, then dressed her in her warmest dress, wrapped a thick shawl around her shoulders, banked up the fire until it roared up the chimney; but still Seraphina's hands were cold as the ice that formed on the windows, her face white as the snow that held the ancient manor house in its chill embrace.

Spiced wine, Megan's potions; nothing could bring back the warmth to Seraphina's body. Her old nurse put her to bed. There were heated bricks at her feet and thick quilts over her, but she felt nothing. It was as if the whole of her being was falling into a strange state between life and death.

Days slipped into weeks. The snow melted from the moors, leaves appeared on the trees. Nothing touched or moved Seraphina. Fearing for her life, Megan summoned the girl's father.

'What you need is that husband of yours. Let him come and give you a good seeing too. That'll bring the blood racing in your veins,' Sir Greville shouted. 'Good grief girl, you were hot and ready enough when young Harry was lifting your petticoats. Brandon's a better man in every respect, so why not send for him?'

Seraphina turned her eyes from the greenish light of her small square of window. 'I don't choose to,' she said, and closed her eyes.

Her father growled something about stubborn-headed women who didn't know what was good for them, then stormed off.

Seraphina's head ached. The hand on her forehead was gentle. Fingers stroked her cheek, curled round her ear. Sliding down the column of her throat, they rested on her collar bone, then down onto the curve of her breast. Warm through the fine linen of her shift, they teased at her nipple. He had come. He had come to her. Just as she had wanted.

A small tremor of pleasure shivered between her legs. Her body loosened. Her hips rose, her breathing quickened. He bent his head. His lips met hers. Soft, boyish lips. Her whole body shuddered with distaste.

'Harry.' Her eyes opened and she saw his worried his

face.

'I thought … Megan, she thought you needed the touch of a man,' he stammered.

Flooded with disappointment, Seraphina turned her head to one side and swallowed back her tears.

'It isn't me you want, is it?'

Seraphina said nothing.

'Do you want me to go?'

'Yes,' she whispered, knowing now that any desire she had ever had for Harry was dead.

She closed her eyes and waited until Harry had disconsolately withdrawn from the room. She remained fond of him, as the companion of her childhood, but could never again feel for him what she once had. Could she in fact feel that for any man? She clenched her fists. A hot wave of fear swept over her. Had the curse she had intended for Brandon rebounded on her? Was she going to be denied her pleasure and satisfaction for the rest of her life?

She sat up. Her head spun. She waited until the room stopped moving, then she pushed back her covers and, holding onto the bedpost, pulled herself to her feet.

'My lady, Seraphina, little one.' As if summoned, Megan hurried into the room. She helped Seraphina into a chair, sent for bread and milk, then warm water to wash.

'Fetch me my scarlet dress,' Seraphina said when she had finished.

'You'll need tighter lacing,' Megan said. 'You are so thin, so wasted. And it's not as warm as the wool.'

'I will wear the silk.' Seraphina lifted her head. Silk was soft and sensuous, it slid over her skin like a lover's touch. A silk dress, the colour of rich red wine; who knew what it might rekindle?

'If you must. But then, it might be for the best.'

'Megan?'

'For your visitor.' The old woman chuckled for the first time since her charge had been taken ill. 'There's someone coming to see you.'

12

Could it be him? Was Brandon finally going to succumb to her will?

Too weak still to pace the room, Seraphina sat on the window seat and gazed through the pitted glass.

Horse's hooves in the stable yard. Voices. She rested her face against the window pane, resisting the urge to fling open the window and call out to him. It would not do. She had summoned him, he had obeyed, and she must not appear too eager.

The door opened. She did not turn. Let him wait those few, final, agonising moments.

'Seraphina.'

It was a woman's voice. Seraphina let out the breath she had been holding, and her heartbeat slowed.

'Artemisia.'

'I hear you have been unwell.' The other woman crossed the room in a rustle of silk and a waft of perfume. 'Here, let me look at you.'

Her hand was soft on Seraphina's shoulder, her touch light. She kissed her neck. Her kiss was gentle, her breath sweet. Seraphina turned and lifted her face. Artemisia smiled. Her lips skimmed Seraphina's.

Seraphina stood up and moved into her arms. Their kisses were hot, insistent, their bodies pressed together.

Artemisia was the first to draw back. 'I did not come for this, delightful though it is. I came because you have been ill, and now that it is spring it is time for you to ride out on the moors with a friend who wishes you nothing but well.' She squeezed Seraphina's hand. 'The air will do you good. It will make you strong again, and when you are strong enough …' She paused and ran her tongue across her lips.

A tremor ran through Seraphina's limbs. Was this the way she would go, into the soft embrace of another woman? But Witchcraven needed an heir. She had to have a daughter or her line would die out. Pushing that thought firmly to the back of her head, Seraphina nodded.

'Tomorrow I will meet you at the Devil's Crown,' Artemisia said.

The thought of going back to the stone circle, where she had last met with the horned god, made Seraphina hesitate.

'Be there,' Artemisia said. 'It is the will of the Goddess,' she added.

Seraphina stared in surprise at her, but she only smiled, kissed her on the lips and was gone.

It was a pale spring morning when Seraphina rode out to the stone circle. A hawk circled overhead in a blue, rain-washed sky. The air was fresh and clean. Seraphina's red dress was loose on her shoulders, her hair felt heavy on her head, but already she could sense the energy returning to her limbs.

She murmured a brief prayer of thanks to the

Goddess as she slipped from Moonlight's back and made her way down the avenue of sunlit stones. She was alone when she reached the centre of the circle. There was no sign of Artemisia. She waited, letting the warmth of the sun seep into her bones, but still Artemisia did not come.

Is she playing with me? Seraphina wondered. *Is this her way of showing that I am nothing but a pawn in some game she has with Brandon?*

Even as the thought crossed her mind, she saw Brandon striding between the stones. He looked pale, thin, his face gaunt and his eyes harrowed. When he saw her, he stopped and frowned, glancing over his shoulder as if expecting someone behind him.

A pulse beat in Seraphina's head. Taking a breath, she stepped forward. 'My lord,' she said. 'I did not think to see you here. I was expecting Artemisia.'

'I too was meeting her. My lady.' He looked at her, his eyes dark with pain.

Seraphina's heart clenched. She had to dig her nails into her palms to stop herself reaching out to him.

'I hear you have been ill.' He moved toward her and stopped.

Seraphina, her mouth dry, nodded.

'I too have been unwell,' he said. 'No, that is not true. I have been very, very sick.'

'Sick?' It was all she could manage, but she knew, just as she was sure he did, the cause of their disease. Megan was right. Artemisia, in bringing them here, was right. They belonged together.

'For pity's sake, Seraphina, let us stop this. Let us simply face the fact that I cannot live without you, and you it seems cannot live without me.'

'Yes.' There was nothing more to say.

'Then what the hell are we going to do about it?'

You could take me, she thought. *Here and now, on the stones, to make our love right in the eyes of the Goddess.* She shook her head. Much as she burned for him, she could not, should not do this. Not now. Not yet.

She stretched out her hand, then dropped it, afraid of what she might do if he touched it. She could see his erection straining through his britches, but he too did not move.

'I think, my lord, that we must wait,' she said.

'Until?' he groaned; but he did not disagree.

'We will know when and why.'

She turned. She wanted to kiss him, to feel his lips on hers, to press herself against the hardness of his cock, but she knew she must not. It took all the strength she could muster, but she walked away, down the avenue of stones to where Moonlight waited beyond their mystical power.

13

Midnight. In her bedroom at Witchcraven, Seraphina slept between fine linen sheets. Her long dark hair spread over the pillows, her eyelashes fluttered, her red lips parted as she dreamed of her midnight lover. The dark, mysterious figure, his eyes passionate and demanding, let his gaze feast on her naked body. His glance lingered on her breasts, the curve of her waist, the slight mound of her stomach, then down to that triangle of dark hair between her thighs.

She woke smiling, threw off her covers and slid out of bed. It was time for the ritual, when she would be with him again. She was naked in the moonlight, her skin white as milk, her hair dark as night, and her nipples rose in the slight chill of the spring air.

She slipped on a white shift and covered it with a dark cloak. Bare-footed she went through the sleeping house, down to the kitchen, where a wreath of blossom waited on the door. Seraphina set the wreath on her head and stepped out into the cobbled yard.

'I am here. I go to worship the Goddess,' she murmured, as two figures appeared out of the darkness.

'We are yours to command, Lady of Witchcraven,'

they replied.

She led them along the upland path, her feet making their way instinctively over the rutted track until they came out onto the dark sweep of the moor. Above them rose the stone circle, its magic drawing into it the power of the moon, so that when she stepped through the ring she entered a dazzling pool of silver light. In its centre stood the altar stone, beside it the priestess, her features masked by the face of an owl. Around her were the worshippers, dark figures that Seraphina could hear but barely see. The men and women who had gathered with their lady to perform the spring ritual.

As she approached, the figures began to chant, slowly at first, then faster, the rhythm beating into her blood, firing her senses. Her cunt grew wet, her hips swayed, her nipples strained against the tightness of her shift.

'My lady.' The priestess fell to her knees before her, and Seraphina let the shift slip from her shoulders. Then the priestess lifted her head and discarded her mask, and Seraphina gave a small gasp of recognition: it was Artemisia!

Artemisia licked out her tongue, lapped around the throbbing clitoris of her lady. Her hands closed around Seraphina's breasts, slid down her back, cupped her buttocks.

Seraphina thrust with her hips, felt the first slow build of orgasm rising within her, but then the lapping ceased, the hands fell away.

It was as it should be. The lady was ready and ripe. It was time.

'Mother and Maiden, Maiden and Crone,' Seraphina prayed, laying her flowers at the foot of the altar. 'Bless our growing time with Your bounty. Make us joyful for the coming of summer, fruitful for the advent of winter.

And for this I offer myself and all around me up to Your pleasure. Come to us, be with us.'

The words swelled round the circle. The light grew more intense, the shadows darker. Black and silver came together in the shape of the horned god. He stood on the altar, magnificent in his nakedness, his erection hard and thick. For her. For her alone.

He was beside her. Hands on her shoulders he faced her. Her body was aflame, burning with a deep sensual need, but a need she knew would be satisfied. She thrust her hips toward him, and he lifted her up. She wound her legs around him, pressing herself against the firmness of his flesh. He lowered her onto the stone, positioned himself above her. His cock brushed her thighs, teased at the lips of her vagina. He bent his head to kiss her. His eyes met hers, and she knew.

'My lady,' he whispered.

'My lord.'

He thrust into her. She closed around him. She smiled. He kissed her. A deep, long, lingering kiss that sent shudders of pleasure to her cunt. Her tongue slid between his lips, tasting him, teasing and yet surrendering. He moved inside her, slowly, steadily. She felt the pleasure build and build so that she was conscious of nothing but their two bodies moving as one. His rhythm quickened, hers too. They were the sun, the moon, the stars. She was on the edge of ecstasy, she was coming, she could not hold back. The universe danced in their coupling, exploded in their pleasure as, with a great cry, they both came.

'My Lady of Witchcraven,' he murmured, cradling her in his arms.

'Lord Brandon,' she sighed with satisfaction. 'Are you truly the horned man?'

'As truly as you are the Lady of Witchcraven. It is what we are called to be, and there is no escaping our destiny.'

'Then we must continue to do our duty.' Seraphina wound her arms around him. 'For without us, my lord, the crops will fail.'

'And the stars fall from the sky,' he murmured, and as the worshippers of the Goddess coupled around them, he thrust once more inside her, completing the age-old ritual of the stones.

ABOUT THE AUTHOR

Kate Dennis is an ex-convent schoolgirl who is fascinated by the supernatural. She loves her husband, champagne, dark chocolate and writing about strong women who are not afraid to break the rules.

When she is not working on a book, she likes to watch films with a dark twist, or gossip with her female friends.

Witchcraven is her first novel.

Romance and Erotica From Telos

ROMANTIC ENCOUNTERS

<u>CATHERINE SERIES BY JULIETTE BENZONI</u>
1: CATHERINE: ONE LOVE IS ENOUGH
2: CATHERINE
3: BELLE CATHERINE (coming soon)
4: CATHERINE: HER GREAT JOURNEY (coming soon)
5: CATHERINE: A TIME FOR LOVE (coming soon)
6: A TRAP FOR CATHERINE (coming soon)
7: CATHERINE: THE LADY OF MONTSALVY (coming soon)

<u>HELEN MCCABE</u>
A GARDEN FAIR (coming soon)
HIGHWAY TO FEAR (coming soon)
HOSTAGE TO LOVE (coming soon)
IN SEARCH OF LOVE (coming soon)
LOVE IN HIDING (coming soon)
THE HOUSE ON THE MOUNTAIN (coming soon)
THE PRICE OF LOVE (coming soon)
WHEN LOVE RIDES OUT (coming soon)

SINFUL PLEASURES

<u>ATHENA MICHAELS</u>
AWAKENING JESSICA

<u>ROBERTA STEELE</u>
BYTE ME!